Arthur W. Beckett, Graham Greene

Fallen among Thieves

a novel of interest

Arthur W. Beckett, Graham Greene

Fallen among Thieves
a novel of interest

ISBN/EAN: 9783337383442

Printed in Europe, USA, Canada, Australia, Japan

Cover: Foto ©Andreas Hilbeck / pixelio.de

More available books at **www.hansebooks.com**

FALLEN AMONG THIEVES.

A Novel of " Interest."

BY

ARTHUR À BECKETT

IN THREE VOLUMES.

VOL. III.

LONDON:

CHAPMAN AND HALL, 193, PICCADILLY.

1870.

FALLEN AMONG THIEVES.

CHAPTER V.

"DOUBT WOULD KILL ME, DARLING."

A MONTH had passed since the interview between Freddy and the detective (narrated in the last chapter of this true and not altogether uneventful history), and most of our *dramatis personæ* were once more at Stelstead. During the month Sir Ralph Ruthven's consent to Leopold's marriage with his ward Florence had been demanded and obtained, and the match had become the talk of the county. The bride's many flirtations, and the bridegroom's numerous thousands, had been discussed over every dinner-table. As Leopold was considered a "new man" by the magnates of the turnip-fields (the country gentlemen I mean), it was thought advisable to arrange a grand *al fresco* ball. At this ball (which was to have been gorgeous in the extreme), the young man was to be introduced to the county, and by them formally "taken up." And at this point I again resume the thread of my story.

Charming weather once more at Stelstead. I am afraid, my dear reader, that you will at length believe that it never rains at this favoured spot, because I always commence my allusion to the little village with wordy descriptions of the rays of the sun. It is not my fault; I protest to you, if ever my Romeo and Juliet are caught in a shower, and are consequently laid up with the influenza, on my word of honour, you shall be duly informed of the terrible disaster.

Stelstead Hall was very full of people. First of all, there were the family,—then

the family's friends, Leopold and his best
man (volunteer), Freddy. Then there were
crowds of carpenters, shoals of cooks, and
loads of servants—all warranted "from London." The sound of preparation was heard
on every side. Some were putting up marquees, others decorating the hall, others
making frames for the splendid display of
fireworks with which the *fête* was to be
brought to a brilliant conclusion. Stelstead
itself was in a *furore* of excitement. The
villagers were mad with joy, and the landlord of the Ruthven Arms was actually
charging as much as two shillings a head for
a single bed. The draper had started a flag
of some unknown country (bought cheap at
the auction of a bankrupt sailor's estate),
which was currently reported to be the
Royal standard of England and Ireland—
especially Ireland—and the baker had deco-
rated his shop windows with a number of
fancy cards, singing the praises of "Taylor's

Hot Cross Buns." From this it will be seen that Stelstead was absolutely wild with delight, and bubbling over with almost frantic revelry.

I am sorry to have to confess it, but to tell the truth, a slight coolness had sprung up between Florence and Leopold. The young man loved his betrothed with all his heart and soul, and Florence seemed very fond of her future husband; but still there was a "something" that marred their joy. The girl was not so demonstrative in her affection as of yore, and seemed almost to dread her lover's eye. The youth was often grave, and seldom smiled. All this and much more had been noted by the attentive Freddy, who rejoiced greatly at the passing(?) shadow, and was exceeding glad.

"I cannot understand it," said Leopold to Edith one day (they often walked together now). "I cannot understand it, but I have a vague presentiment of coming sorrow."

"Sorrow!" she replied, looking up into his face. "What have you to do with sorrow? Why, the whole world is before you. You are young, and love and are beloved."

"Are you sure of that?"

"Quite sure."

They walked on in silence under the trees, and towards the river's bank. As they neared the water, the sound of voices in earnest conversation caught their ears. The sound was so soft, that it seemed only a murmur of trinkling wavelets.

Edith stopped suddenly, and turned pale. Leopold, seeing her white face, moved towards her with anxious eyes, and outstretched arms.

"It is nothing," she murmured faintly; "I shall be better soon. Come, let us go along that avenue."

She would have walked away, but now it was Leopold's turn to pause. He looked into her eyes, and as the dark, long lashes shielded them from his inquiring glance, strode towards the river.

"Stay," she cried; "do not go that way."

He put her gently from him, and walked on. "Have no fear," he said, and pushed back the branches with his hand.

He stood before them.

Florence rushed towards him, fell into his arms, and burst out crying.

"Don't, my darling, don't," he said in a kindly soothing voice. "I do not doubt you, love, for if I doubted you, it would kill me!"

He stood with her thus, and his arms seem to shield her from the world. Then he turned round, and sternly confronted her companion.

With an apology to the ladies for smoking, Freddy quietly lighted a cigarette.

CHAPTER VI.

FREDDY MAKES A FALSE MOVE.

LEOPOLD kissed Florence's forehead, and gently led her to Edith. It was a strange sight to watch the two girls as they stood together. The first stern and solemn and dark, the other tearful, bowed down with shame, and fair;—like unto the thundercloud one—like unto the wind-driven lakewater the other. Edith received her sister and soothed her; still like the mother and child; but only for a moment, for then she turned away and addressed Leopold.

"For Heaven's sake be calm !" she whispered, "for her sake !" and she pointed to Florence, who stood alone and in tears.

"Have no fear," said the young man, in the cold, passionless tone that at one time was habitual to him,—that tone so well remembered by Edith, recalling to her the hopeless, faithless traveller on board the 'Queen of the West.' "Have no fear. See to your sister, and leave us alone."

He held out his hand, and as Edith clasped it within her own she found it as cold and as clammy as the hand of a corpse. She looked at his face; it was as pale as marble, and as rigid, save about the mouth, where the lips trembled—trembled, but only a little.

"Go with Edith, darling, I will soon follow you;" he said with an effort, and the two girls left him.

He stood watching them as they passed out of sight. When the bushes hid them

from his view, he turned round and confronted Freddy. That charming individual
was rather white about the cheeks. Perhaps
his pallor might have been attributed to his
cigarette, and yet the dear boy was an in-
veterate smoker.

"Ta, ta, old man," said Holston, with an
affectation of unconcern; "I'm off—I think
I shall take my gun, and look after the partridges."

There was something almost absurd about
this speech; it was so *very* like Cox's pro-
posal to Box "to take a stroll." If you and
I, dear reader, had been there we should
have laughed outright, but then *we* (at least
I speak for myself) are *not* in love with
Florence Ruthven.

"Stay!" said Leopold calmly, but sternly,
"I want a word with you."

"As you will," cried Freddy, with a little
laugh, and he threw himself on the grass,
and lighted a fresh cigarette. "Nothing

gives me greater pleasure than a chat with you—you are always amusing."

Leopold looked at the figure lying before him for a second or so, and then murmured, "He is young, and youth is generous; I will try him."

As for Freddy, he puffed away at his cigarette with great assiduity.

"Holston," began Leopold, "when I came to England I hadn't a friend in the world, you know that. We have seen a good deal of each other, and, as far as two men of the nineteenth century *can* be friends, we have been friends."

"Quite so, dear boy," said Freddy, with something very like a sigh of relief. "You smoke,—have a cigarette?"

Leopold sat down, and accepted mechanically the proffered courtesy.

"When I came down here," he continued, "I came for a purpose. Pardon my frankness, but it was to save Florence Ruthven from contracting a marriage which I knew could only lead to misery. I came here to prevent Florence Ruthven from becoming your wife."

"Thanks, very much."

"I knew that you did not love her; I knew that you did not care for her even as much as the ballet girl whose portrait you still wear in that locket on your watch chain."

"Wrong, my dear boy, I changed the portrait more than a week ago for another. Quite a correct person this time;" he opened the locket as he spoke, but, after glancing at Leopold's stern pale face and hard clenched hands, closed it again.

"You would laugh at me," continued Leopold, "if I told you that I came to save this poor girl from a wretched future out of pure philanthropy."

"Not at all."

"No; it was a selfish motive that brought

me here. It matters not when, but once upon a time Florence Ruthven was (as now) betrothed to me."

"You had seen her before you met down here?" cried Freddy, in accents of surprise.

"Yes. I thought my love was dead; I thought that I might safely be near her without feeling a revival of affection. I came here to save a grave from desecration, —to keep an old memory undefiled."

"Thanks awfully for the kind, what do you call it,—simile, isn't it?"

"But I was wrong; I had miscalculated my strength; my old feelings revived, my old love returned."

"I am sure your story is most interesting," said Freddy; "but, really, if you have nothing else to say I think, perhaps, as the end of your little history can keep, you know, and we can't always have fine weather, that I had better seize this opportunity of blazing away at the partridges."

"I have something more to say," continued Leopold, in the calm cold tone with
which he had spoken from the first during
this interview, "and I wish to be quite
frank with you. We are both young, and—
but there, what I wish to say is this,—Florence Ruthven is my affianced wife, and I
love her as only a man can love once in his
life; it would kill my soul to think that she
did not return my affection."

"Don't think it then, my boy."

"I have been long enough in England to
have heard stories of your life, Holston, and
I know it is in your power to persecute any
woman who may cross your path."

"Really, my dear fellow, you seem to
know my character to a tittle."

"I wish to deal honestly with you, Holston; and as man to man: I don't want to
threaten,—a lady's name should never be
mixed up with a brawl. More than this, I
would rather trust to your generosity than
rely on your fear."

"Thanks, very much. You are really very good."

"You have it in your power to distress Florence by your attentions. You have it in your power to persecute her. She is my wife before Heaven, and this must not be."

"Quite so."

"My faith in Florence is unbounded."

"Quite so;" this time with a slight sneer.

"Well, if you will, I am a coward! God pardon me, but I do *so* fear to lose my jewel of price—my ray of sunshine, that I dare scarcely believe in Heaven itself. Leave us alone, Holston; do not attempt to sow the seeds of sorrow and doubt in our hearts. Be generous; you owe me some reparation for the past; make your reparation thus."

"Owe you reparation!" Again Freddy spoke in accents of surprise.

Leopold was silent. Freddy waited for a moment; then he lighted a fresh cigarette, cleared his throat, glanced sideways at his companion, and began,

"You've been frank, very frank with me, Richard Harwood, and I will follow the fashion, and be equally frank with you."

He paused for a moment, as if he had anything but a pleasant task before him, and rather shrank from the duty that had been forced upon him. This hesitation over, and he continued,

"You've said that we are both men of the world, and you are right; but you left out a distinction. You should have added, that whereas I am a deuced poor man of the world, you are an uncommonly rich one."

Leopold was silent, but his face reflected surprise and curiosity. Without looking at him, Holston went on half defiantly and half timorously,

"You've said, with some truth, that I don't care, and never did care, a very great deal for Florence Ruthven. The lady isn't here, and so I drop my gallantry, and admit the fact without reservation. I don't care for her more than I care for any other jolly girl with pretty features and a nice figure."

Lawson made a movement of impatience.

"Beg pardon, old fellow," said Freddy, observing this demonstration, "I didn't want to offend you, but I thought frankness was to be the order of the day, and I'm only frank. Well then, as a man of the world, I will put love and passion, and all that stuff, out of the question. I get my love, as you have hinted, like flowers from Covent Garden, and it grows, ripens, and dies at St. John's Wood. It's merely a question of bracelets and broughams. Love and sixty per cent., separation and the sponging-house."

And he paused for a moment, laughed, tugged at his tawny moustache, and continued,—

"You have also been good enough to hint

at something else equally true, I regret to say. I have it in my power to be disagreeable, more disagreeable than you imagine. Now the question is, shall I be disagreeable or shall I not?"

Leopold was quite silent, but his breath came a little faster than its wont. He turned away from Freddy and clenched his fist. Holston glanced at him sharply and said slowly and with an affectation (mind you, only an affectation) of *sang froid*,

"Now, I am a poor man and you are rich. I believe in equality, and am a fearful democrat. I reason to myself why should all the money be in one man's pocket? Why indeed? Is it not the duty of every poor man to attempt to obtain a fairer distribution? Unquestionably. By any means? Certainly by any means."

He paused for a moment and laughed. But, to tell the truth, the laugh was a little forced.

"Well," he began again, "to be quite frank. I only wanted Florence Ruthven for her money. You have got the start of me, and I don't mind giving up the race if you will help me (in a delicate, gentlemanly manner) to carry out my great idea of distributing wealth with a little greater regard to equality. For instance, let us begin with ourselves,—you are a rich man and I a poor one. What do you say?"

Leopold had risen from the ground, but he did not answer. Freddy followed his example and continued,—

"It is only just that you should know what advantages you will gain by this little scheme. By good fortune I have a weapon that I can use against the uncle. Sir Ralph Ruthven is in my power. As men of the world we both of us can see that it is possible (girls are so silly, you know), that it is possible, I repeat, that the niece may step in to save the uncle. Now, five thousand pounds with your wealth is very little to you; and yet if you were to pay the sum in to my bankers, you would assist very greatly in bringing to pass my pet scheme of pecuniary equality for all men. What do you say ?"

"What do I say!" thundered out Leopold, trembling with passion and indignation. "Why, this. I will give you just half an hour to pack up and leave this house, and if you are not gone by that time—"

"Well?"

"I will kick you out of the place with the thickest boots I can find, and supplement the attention with as sound a horse-whipping as you ever had in your life!"

Leopold drew out his watch, marked the time, and then with an expression of supreme contempt turned on his heel and walked leisurely away.

And what was Freddy doing?

Nothing! He was as white as a sheet, and trembled like an aspen. Help me to laugh at him, reader, as he stands there like a beaten cur. And yet it is a painful sight. Those few unresented words of Leopold had deprived Freddy of all his manhood, all his self-respect. He was a coward! Good heavens, a paltry miserable coward! Look at his contorted features, at his trembling lips. Stay, though,—turn away, for pity's sake turn away,—the poor cur is crying! For the moment I really feel for him,—it is *so* painful to see manhood dethroned, to listen to the sobbing of a degraded fellow-creature.

Freddy's emotion did not last for long. He soon regained his calmness.

"Thank God," he murmured, "no one overheard him. After all, what does it matter?"

He walked away with a clouded face, stopping every moment to ponder.

" I have been a fool," he cried at last, " a
stupid, clumsy fool.   I have shown my cards
and lost the game."

He walked on in the direction of Stelstead.
As he passed through the park gates, he
looked in at the lodge and requested that
his servant might be found and told to join
him at the Ruthven Arms.   Then he continued his journey.

In due course he arrived at the inn.   He
ordered a bed, and sat in the coffee-room.
Then he asked for some note-paper and an
envelope.   After a few minutes' delay they
were carried in to him by his servant, who,
to tell the truth, had been drinking at the
bar when summoned to attend upon his
master.

" I shall sleep here to-night," said Freddy.
"Just go up to the Hall and pack up my
things and bring them here."

" Yes, Sir," rejoined the man, without
showing the slightest astonishment at the
order.

"I shall have a letter for you to carry. Look in before you go."

"Yes, Sir."

"I have failed with him," murmured Freddy when the man had left the room. "My remaining chance is with her;" and then he took up his pen, thought for a moment, and began writing.

"Give this to Miss Florence," said he, when his servant returned; "you need not let any one know about it. You understand."

The man bowed and left the room.

"There," he murmured, when he was once more alone; "I have done my best—the rest I must leave to the devil!"

You see he alluded to the spirit of evil—a fact that proves that his religious education had not been neglected.

CHAPTER VII.

" POOR DEAR LEOPOLD ! "

EDITH and Florence returned to the house
almost in silence. They passed through
the park with its wide-spreading trees and
autumn-tinged leaves, its yellowish grass
and tangled brushwood; over the lawn,
where the labourers were at work erecting
the frames for the fire-works ordered for the
quickly approaching *fête*; past the site of
the old Raymond murder, across the terrace,
and into the house.

" Father Dutton is here, Miss," said a
servant to Edith as the two girls entered.

"I have shown him into the drawing-room."

"Tell him, please, that I will be with him directly." The man walked away to do her bidding as she left the hall and ascended the staircase. After a few minutes she proceeded to the apartment into which the priest had been shown, entered the room, and gave him welcome.

"I am so glad you have come, Mr. Dutton," she said. "You received my note?"

"And am here in consequence. But first, how are your uncle and sister? I have not seen Miss Florence for an age. Is the day fixed for the happy event?"

A shadow passed over Edith's face as he said this. She spoke calmly, however.

"I believe for the end of next month. My uncle is tolerably well, and as for Florence, I expect her down soon and then she will be able to speak for herself."

There was an awkward pause here, and then Edith continued,—

"I sent to you, Mr. Dutton, because I wished to ask your advice. I am living in a world of difficulties, and know not what to do? The responsibility that has been thrust upon me is more than I can bear. Will you, honest, noble-hearted gentleman that you are, help me to bear it?"

"Most assuredly," replied the priest. "You may rely on my best services, Miss Ruthven."

"I can trust you implicitly,—nothing will make you reveal what I am about to tell you?"

"I have had the honour of wearing her Majesty's uniform," said the priest, tugging at an imaginary moustache, "and—"

"Pardon me," interrupted Edith with a blush, "but I have been so deceived that I can scarcely trust any one. You have forgiven me?"

" My daughter,—I beg pardon, I should say Miss Ruthven," murmured the worthy Father, already ashamed of his show of wrath. " You have given me no cause for anger."

" Thanks, a thousand thanks," said Edith, " and now I will speak unreservedly. You remember the night of Emma Barlow's death ?"

The priest inclined his head.

" You remember the conversation that passed between that woman and my uncle? Yes, I see you do. Well, I have discovered the secret hidden from us on that dreadful night."

" What !" exclaimed the priest, " have you found Sir Ralph's son—your cousin ?"

" Yes. And my discovery troubles me sorely, oh, so sorely. Promise me that you will consider the story I am about to narrate as sacred as the secrets of your own confessional, and you will indeed deserve my gratitude."

"I promise," replied the priest, with a slight tug at his imaginary moustache.

And then Edith began. It was a long story, and a story that moved Father Dutton strangely,—a story that I shall tell myself ere I lay down my pen and bid adieu to my readers. The priest turned very pale as the narrative was brought to a conclusion, —he turned pale, I say, and trembled.

"What shall I do?" cried Edith when her tragic tale was over; "what shall I do? I dare not tell him, knowing what he knows. Tell me, Father Dutton, what shall I do?"

The priest was silent for a minute, rapt in deep, deep thought, and then he said,—

"My daughter, let the dead bury the dead. Bury your secret in Emma Barlow's grave."

Shortly after this, Father Dutton took his leave, and Edith was left alone.

"Yes, it is better that it should be so,"

murmured the girl, as she looked drearily
out on the park as the sunshine faded into
twilight, "but how hard it is to live!"—

> "I am weary, I am weary,
>   I would that I were dead!"

She turned aside and took up a book, and
tried to read, but the letters had for her no
meaning, her mind was carried far, far away
by her thoughts.

"Edith!" said a soft timid voice, "I
want to speak to you."

She looked up quickly, almost angrily,
from the volume she held in her hands, and
found her sister standing before her.

"You, Florence!"

"Yes, Edith. But first let me get this
footstool, and put it here. And now let me
kneel—so."

Edith sat near one of the large old windows, with the light streaming down upon
her robe, but with her face in deep shadow.
Florence knelt beside her, with her arms

resting upon her sister's lap, with clasped hands and tearful eyes.

"You won't be angry with me?"

Edith stooped down, and kissed her sister's forehead.

"No, dear, I will not be angry with you."

"Edith, I don't know what is the matter with me, I believe I am going mad!"

Strange words, and passionate. The girl uttered them defiantly, and then burst out crying. Edith soothed her.

"Don't, darling, don't. Surely *you* have no cause for tears. You should be so happy."

"But I am not. I am sure he doesn't care for me. I believe he hates me."

A qualm of pain passed over Edith's face as she replied,

"Florence, Florence, don't speak like that! You know, you *must* know, that Leopold loves you, and you only."

"I dare not believe it; you hear, Edith, I *dare* not believe it!"

" You dare not believe it !"

The elder sister spoke with fear and surprise. Her face became cold and white for
a moment, and then she started, as if some
thought had entered her mind which was too
horrible for meditation.

" You dare not believe it !"

" No, Edith ! I don't know what has
come to me lately, but I feel so—so wretched ! I feel that I—that I—"

" Well ?"

" You know he had not seen me for five
years, and I am so frivolous and flighty;
and Freddy Holston came, and he is such a
flirt, and—"

" Well ?"

" Don't look at me like that, Edith !
What—what have I done ? I am sure it is
not my fault. One can't force oneself to
love at will. And Freddy is certainly so
amusing, and dresses so well, and Leopold's
moody, and I am sure doesn't care for me,
although you say he does, and—"

" Well ?"

" Oh, I don't know,". said Florence, with a passionate burst of weeping, " I am afraid to think. Since Freddy's been here I have lost my love, for—you know what I would say. I don't, I can't love him."

" You don't love him !"

Edith had risen from the window, and had cast Florence from her. She stood in the twilight, stern and as cold and as motionless as a statue.

" You don't love him, and you dare to tell me this !" she cried indignantly ; " to tell me ! who've sacrificed my own happiness in life for yours. *You* dare to tell *me* this !"

" Oh, Edith !" murmured Florence, looking up into her sister's face appealingly ; " forgive me, and don't look like that at me."

" Don't touch me ! Miserable girl, you have wrecked your own happiness ; you have laid up a future of regret and misery. You know what a sacrifice I made for you; and now you tell me, when my heart is dead, you dare to tell me that you don't love him! Don't come near me! Let me go, I say, your very touch is contamination!" And she swept out of the room with the dignity of an offended goddess, leaving her sister kneeling and crying on the floor.

A pretty picture indeed! Painful in its way; you know my objection to tears, and a woman weeping is a particularly unpleasant sight. But then it is not my fault, dear reader. Have I not warned you that I cannot paint a lie? Have I not told you that Florence is not my *beau idéal* of womanly excellence? *Entre nous*, womanly excellence resembles the tales we used to learn at school about Jupiter and Juno, Cupid and Psyche,—very pretty, but not altogether unmythical. It may be that women are angels in heaven (who thinks of a male angel?), because they are devils on earth. If Florence disappoints you, believe me,—she has disappointed me.

Of course, she was very grieved at the "scene" that had just taken place. She loved her sister, in her flighty way, as much as she loved anything or anybody upon earth. She was not only grieved but angry. With whom do you think, dear reader? Why, with poor unoffending Leopold; with the man she had wronged, with the lover she had deceived! So angry was she with him, that her rage half excused (in her mind) her perfidy.

" Oh," she said at last, when her tears had dried, " he will make me hate him !"

And then, with woman's beautiful, logical nature, her thoughts flew to the other end of the pole, and she grew maudlin over " poor dear Leopold !"

And we marry this kind of people !

CHAPTER VIII.

FALSE MOVE—NUMBER TWO.

" Not at all bad wine, landlord," said Freddy. He was in great spirits, and had just finished dinner. It was about eight o'clock, and he held in his hand a letter written in a female's scrawl. "Not at all bad wine. Claret, eh ?"

" Well, Sir," replied the host of the Ruthven Arms, scratching his head, " I've no doubt but what you say, Sir, is quite correct, still I always thought that that there wine was port, Sir."

" Why, bless my soul !" cried Freddy,

sipping his glass, "and now I come to taste it, so it is. Any one could see that this was meant for port."

For all that, Holston put down his glass with a shiver, that might have meant either contempt for the good things of this world or disgust at the vintage of the beverage he had just imbibed.

"To let you into a secret, Sir," whispered the landlord confidentially, "I'm far from pleased with them foreign wines. I've said many a time to my missus that I would make my own wine. Our home-brewed beer is very good, I says to my missus; then, why not try our home-brewed wine?"

"Quite so. And what does your 'missus' say to you?"

"Well, Sir, to tell you the truth, she's a little quaint. When I talks about it she calls me a fool."

Freddy laughed lightly at the landlord's idea of quaintness, and said,

"By the bye, do you know Mr. Dutton, the Roman Catholic priest?"

"Oh, yes, Sir; he is very well known over here. He's got only one enemy in Stelstead, the butcher; my wife says the butcher hates him because he doesn't eat meat on a Friday, but, as I've explained before, my wife's a little quaint."

"I suppose he's very much like other men; he's got his price. These Papists are very fond of the money-bags, eh?"

"Well, so they say, Sir; not that I've ever found Mr. Dutton a miser. He gives away a deal of money to that Catholic family down at Barker's End. My only objection to him is, he's rather too fond of converting people as he calls it. He's been at my wife, and tried very hard to convert her."

"With any success?"

"Oh, dear no, Sir; my wife's a match for any Papist in the kingdom,—she's so quaint. They got jabbering about the infallibility of the Church; and when she heard that females aren't admitted to the general councils, she said that it was impossible for the Church to be in the right,—that no one but a woman *could* be infallible."

"And did he attempt to convert you?"

"Yes, Sir, he did a little; but he found me very unpromising. You see, Sir, when I was nine years old they gave me a prize at school for Scripture history—Paley's 'Evidences of Christianity.' I am sorry to say I read it, Sir, and I have not been able to quite believe in anything ever since. My wife, when her temper is ruffled, has a funny little way of throwing the castors at me. On these occasions she has frequently alluded to me as a Deist."

"From what you tell me, I should imagine that Mr. Dutton must be an enthusiast."

"That's just what he is, Sir. He won't leave people alone. He and Mr. Hardway, the minister at the Dissenting chapel, have ruined half my customers."

"Ruined!"

"Yes, Sir. Before them parsons interfered, all my customers used to get 'comfortable' regularly every Saturday night, and now I haven't seen more than a couple of dozen or so of them drunk for the last fortnight!"

"Really! Will you kindly send me my coffee now?"

"Yes, Sir; certainly, Sir. What I hold, Sir, is this," said the landlord, opening the door, and preparing to take his departure; "if mankind ain't intended to get 'toxicated, why on earth do we have beer? · Why it stands to reason, and it's rank nonsense to say otherwise. Even my wife agrees with me about this, and she *is* a quaint one!"

The coffee was brought in due time, and duly discussed.

When Freddy was left alone, he pulled

at his tawny moustache, and murmured, "An enthusiast, eh? Well, I can't lose *much* credit in this part of the country now; and after all, it's worth the trial. It certainly would suit my book uncommonly well if I could manage it. On my soul I'm becoming quite a melodramatic villain! How I shall laugh at all this when it's over!"

He took up his hat, looked once more at the letter he held in his hand, opened the door, and walked out.

Father Dutton was smoking a cigar and reading the 'Pall Mall Gazette.' His work was over for the day, and he was enjoying a couple of hours of recreation before retiring to rest.

"Legarde sold out!" said he, laying down the paper. "Ah, how all the old fellows are leaving the regiment! If I showed up at mess now, scarcely a man would recognize me."

And he continued puffing at his cigar, and pondering over the past.

It was a pleasant room enough. Certainly poor, but as certainly neat. A few books (among them conspicuous the red-covered 'Army List'), a pair of foils, a cavalry sword, and a fishing-rod, attracted the attention of those who entered the apartment. Besides these, there were the usual religious articles common to the house of a Roman Catholic priest,—a crucifix, a small altar, a reading-desk, and a large Bible.

When his cigar was half burned out, an old woman entered the room, and said,

"If you please, Father, here's a gentleman at the door who says he wants to speak to you on particular business,—on religious business, he says."

The priest took the card held out to him, and when he had read the name inscribed upon it, gave a start of genuine surprise.

"H'm!" he murmured; "well, I don't

understand this, but I suppose I had better see him. Show him in, please, Mrs. Tomkins."

The aged housekeeper retired, and returned ushering in Mr. Frederick Holston.

"Sorry to disturb you, Mr. Dutton, but I wanted to see you particularly,—on *private* business," and he glanced meaningly at the venerable female who still remained in the room.

"You can leave us, Mrs. Tomkins," said the priest, taking the hint. "And now, Sir, what do you want with me at this hour of the night?"

As he uttered this, there was a good deal more of the plunger about the Reverend Dutton than the priest, and he looked absolutely fierce as he regarded his visitor.

"My dear Sir, I've got some good news for you," answered Freddy, taking a chair without any invitation. "You will be glad to learn that I am converted to Roman Catholicism."

" Congratulate yourself, Sir,—not us."

" Eh !" exclaimed Freddy, with great surprise ; "do you mean to say that all of you will not be delighted to hear the news ?"

" Your name will be added to beggars and nobles. We don't classify converts. But you didn't come to tell me this, I presume ?"

If the ground had opened before him, and shown a hole to the other side of the earth, Freddy could not have looked more surprised. He had expected to find a weak enthusiast, and, lo and behold, he had to deal with a stern, clear-headed man of the world ! He was silent for a moment, and then burst out laughing.

" Serves me right; it serves me thoroughly right !" he cried; "of course it would be much better to deal frankly with you. Your retort, Mr. Dutton, is quite refreshing."

" I'm glad you like it."

"I do, upon my word. Now come, I see we are both men of the world, and can meet each other on an equality. Between ourselves, you can be useful to me, and I think I can be useful to you. Shall I go on?"

"As you. please," said the priest carelessly; but he still stood and tapped on the floor with his foot, impatiently.

"To tell you the truth," continued Freddy, "I don't go in very heavily for religion. If I had my choice, I think I should rather like to be a Mahometan, or a very great swell indeed among the Buddhists, but Roman Catholicism does very well for me just now. I want to be married."

"You can come to me about that in the morning. It's late now, and—"

"The morning won't do," interrupted Freddy. "To tell you the truth, I want to get a girl to elope with me. She has plenty of money, and—"

"Well?"

"I had better be frank with you," said

the young man with a laugh. "Now I know
you gentlemen in the cassock."

"Oh, you know us, do you?"

"Down to the ground, Sir. Now, as you
have asked me to come to the point and not
to beat about the bush, I may as well out
with it at once. I am deuced poor, and this
will be a very great catch. She's awfully
spoony upon me, and I'm sure I can get her
to come. However, to smooth away her
objections and to make it all right (I really
want to marry her, you know), I thought,
perhaps, you might assist us and tie the knot.
I *did* intend to have worked upon your feelings as a devout convert, but you, by your
most excellent sense, have saved me from
perpetrating such a very purposeless piece of
tomfoolery."

"Well," said Father Dutton with a very
ominous tug at his imaginary moustache.

"Oh, only this," continued Freddy, regardless of the coming storm. "I know

Roman Catholicism very well, and Roman Catholic priests even better. I know that money in your (I beg pardon), in *our* church, can buy anything, from absolution for a sanguinary murder down to permission to commit a fine healthy burglary. Now, as a rule, a little matter like a hurried marriage costs scarcely anything; but as I am no niggard, I have no objection to pay if you will perform the ceremony,—a tenner to St. Anybody-you-please and a fiver for yourself. Pardon me for putting the matter a little coarsely, but in matters of business it is just as well to be explicit. You see I am a Roman Catholic, and so you have a capital excuse for your conduct. Well, is St. Anybody-you-please to have his candles or is he not? What do you say?"

"Why, simply this," said the priest striding to the door and throwing it open; " get out of my house at once,—at once, do you hear, or I shall forget my cloth and strike you?"

" Eh, come, come, Mr. Dutton," ejaculated Freddy in the last stage of astonishment, "you know a joke's a joke, and if a tenner isn't enough—"

"Stop, I tell you,—get up, how dare you sit in my presence?" cried the priest at the top of his voice, and then he crossed himself, seemed to swallow something in his throat, and said in a mild voice, "Please go away before I forget that I am a man of peace."

Freddy rose and approached the door. When he got there he turned round and said, "Mr. Dutton, if I have made a mistake—"

"Don't speak to me or I shall knock you down!" shouted the clergyman, and then he added in a mild voice and after another crossing as he opened the street door, "I beg your pardon,—good night."

"I shall never make a good priest," said the worthy man as he returned to his study, "never, never, never! I am such a very hopeless subject," and he was quite depressed.

As for Freddy he thought to himself, " What a fool I am ! It serves me right for entertaining such romantic ideas. Who wants a marriage in these days ? the world can do very well without them, at least for a fortnight. In spite of all this I shall gain the day." He looked at the letter to which reference has already been made, " Nine o'clock at the rustic bridge. It's time to go. H'm, my visit to that idiot of a priest was a false move. False move No. 2 ; confound it."

CHAPTER IX.

THE FIREWORKS AT STELSTEAD.

THE night of the ball at last arrived. The carpenters had put the finishing touches to the marquees, the gaunt framework of the fireworks stood out in bold relief against the evening sky, and all was ready for the reception of the guests; the candles were lighted, the musicians had taken up their places in the drawing-room, and the supper waited merry discussion in the library.

Florence was in her bedroom, busy about her head-dress. I am not learned in ladies' dresses, but I believe she was charmingly attired. She wore a light blue robe, made of some gauzy material, with a turquoise locket, and blue flowers in her hair *en suite*. She was flushed with excitement, and certainly looked very beautiful. After a finishing touch from the hands of her maid, she tripped down the staircase, and was ready in the hall to welcome her uncle's guests.

The " County " came.

Old family coaches rolled up the avenue and past the lodge, with flashing lamps and galloping horses. More modern vehicles followed suit, to be followed again by dog-carts and traps of every description. Soon the rooms in the old hall were alive with colour. Jewels sparkled, silk and satin rustled, and bouquets gave forth a grateful fragrance.

A motley company,—dowagers in paint and diamonds, with grinning skulls and wrinkled throats, as proud as Lucifer and twice as disagreeable. These amiable ladies retired to the rout-seats ranged round the room, and employed their time in keeping a sharp look-out upon their daughters, and in killing reputations from behind their fans.

Then there were "frisky matrons" rejoicing in the first liberty of early marriage; plump and lively, with a turn for sentiment, and a decided taste for champagne. They danced with frantic energy, and languished with great perseverance,—in fact, were just the kind of people that their children would not like to have recognized as their mothers!

Then there were maidens. Such sweet creatures! Some in nice, pretty dresses, making up for in train what they lacked in body. Lovely beings! all heart and innocence, and so versatile. So very sentimental with Spoony, the Ensign of the 10th, and so particularly "wicked" with Cavendish of the K. D. G. Amiable and "experienced" females,—this ball belonged to their eighth season.

Then there were other maidens.   Poor
women who had come to that time of life
when rice powder is a necessary, and rouge
scarcely a luxury,—women who grinned
their best and looked their youngest, in the
faint hope of yet saving themselves from the
fearful future awaiting those who do not
marry before they are five-and-thirty.

Again, there were others.   Girls just
"out."   Really timid, and really enjoying
themselves,—catching a glimpse of heaven
in a waltz—a shadow of paradise in a galop.
Girls who next year would be hurried
through a course of London life, until they
had lost their health, hearts, and innocence.

And now for the men.   A good many
soldiers,—stupid but agile, with heavy moustaches and much conceit.   There was a
cavalry regiment stationed not very far from
Stelstead, and the barracks sent forth a strong
detachment to the ball.   Not bad fellows in
their way, these plungers.   If you would

only subscribe to their creed,—"there's only one institution in the world,—the British Army, and the —— Light Dragoons is its prophet,"—you would be sure of gaining their favour. Hospitable to a degree, and *au fond* kind-hearted. Rather too much swagger, perhaps, for some tastes ; but not a black heart in a score of them.

Then there were swell young civil servants from London, who had been " brought " by the people with whom they had been staying. Conceited and foppish, with a great contempt for the military and an overwhelming respect for themselves. They did not dance much, but some of them were rather clever at flirting. Besides the civil and military, there were the "county" young men,—the heirs to baronetcies and landed property, and these were those most in favour with the gushing old dowagers already referred to.

Sir Ralph stood near the door, bowing to

his guests. The old man was very pale, and looked about the room with an uneasy glance, as if he expected some unwelcome visitor who would not be denied admittance. Edith was near him, and tried to comfort him.

"You are not well, uncle," she said; "why don't you go and lie down, dear? This noise and confusion is too much for you."

"Lie down," he echoed, looking into her face vacantly. "In the dark? No, no, no; I hate the dark," he whispered; "I am afraid of the dark!"

He passed his hand through his hair, and murmured, "What am I saying? Ah, Edith, I'm better now,—much better."

The music struck up for the opening quadrille, and Leopold led Florence out to dance.

"You look very well to-night, dear," he whispered, as they passed along to the head of the room.

" Oh, Leopold, don't be so silly !" she said, with a blush of anger.

Lawson did not reply, and the dance commenced ; when it was over, they walked away, and at last found themselves in the conservatory.

" Florence, what is the matter ?"

" Nothing !" she replied pettishly ; and she played with her bouquet, and would not look up into his face.

" Something has separated us of late, Florence. Something—I know not what. Why has this change come over you ?"

" I know of no change."

" Florence !"

" You weary me ! Ah ! here you are, Captain Lofton. Yes, the first waltz is yours ;" and she sailed away on the arm of the new-comer.

Leopold stood quite still, and felt a sinking at his heart. He bit his lips, and thought, " Why should I find fault with her? She is young, and my youth was so long, long ago."

He walked out of the conservatory into the fresh night air. As he strolled away under the branches, he imagined he saw the shadow of a man falling from behind one of the trees. He walked on briskly, and soon reached the spot.

" You here?"

" Yes," said Freddy, for Freddy it was; " and why not? I have received a card. Don't say you have seen me, because I don't intend to show up,—I've got such a con- founded headache."

" I wonder you dare to come within a hun- dred yards of me after our last interview."

" Oh, Harwood, you take things too seriously. I forget what you said now."

" I do not. Shall I repeat the words?"

" No, thanks; for I remember you were exceedingly disagreeable. But there, I bear no malice. Here is my hand."

Lawson looked at it contemptuously. " You are impertinent," he said, and walked away.

" Ah, my fine fellow," murmured Freddy, as Leopold disappeared, " you may insult me now as much as you please. To-night, dear boy, I get at your heart."

And he still waited behind the tree.

Leopold, wrapped in thought, wandered about hither and thither, stopping to listen every now and then to the gay sound of the dance-music. By-and-by he returned to the ball-room to look for Florence. She was not there.

He walked among the dancers, who were now promenading, and soon encountered Edith, engaged in lively conversation with a cornet of dragoons.

" At eleven o'clock you say, Miss Ruth-ven ?"

" At eleven o'clock, and then we shall come back to supper."

"Oh, I'm so glad you're going to have fireworks," said the youthful plunger. "I do so like them, they are so very pretty."

"Have you seen your sister, Edith?" asked Leopold, approaching them.

"Always Florence, Leopold," said Edith with a smile. "No, I've not seen her for the last ten minutes. I am afraid you neglect her sadly. Why, you have only had one dance with her the whole evening."

And with a friendly nod the fair girl moved away, and once more attempted to take a civil interest in her partner's in-anities.

Leopold continued his search. He returned to the park. As he walked along the terrace, he heard the rustle of a silk dress, and a voice say in low tones, "Twelve o'clock—I will not be later than twelve o'clock."

"Some happy couple, I suppose," thought Leopold with a smile; "how selfish we are!

Why here am I so wrapped up in my own love, that I cannot understand a flirtation in others."

He sat down on one of the seats, and looked out across the moonlit country.

"What a beautiful night!" he said; "the fireworks will be a success."

He rested his head upon his hand and continued,—

"What ails Florence to-night, I wonder? Her manner is quite changed to me. Perhaps I was in fault. I am so fond of her that I may be too demonstrative. Well, all lovers have their quarrels. If they did not, how could they ever know the pleasure of reconciliation? Yes, yes, I was in the wrong. I will return to the ball-room and try to find her."

This time his search was crowned with success. He met Florence at the entrance of the conservatory.

"Can you spare me a moment, my dear?"

he said kindly ; and she followed him
in.

"Florence," he began, when they were
both seated on the sofa, "I was silly this
evening to bother you. I am very sorry.
I am nervous and stupid; but you know
why."

She trembled as if she were cold, and yet
the weather was very warm for September.

"You mustn't be angry with me, my
darling," he continued, "if the slightest
change in your manner worries me. You
don't, you never will know how dear, how
very dear you are to me."

"Oh, don't speak to me like that," cried
Florence ; and the tears gathered in her
eyes. "Don't speak kindly to me, Leopold.
I do not deserve it. I cannot—I cannot
bear it."

Leopold gazed at her with a glance full of
surprise.

"Not speak kindly to you, Florence ?"

"Oh, Leopold, if you only knew all !" she said, with a sob. "But promise me, dearest, promise me one thing," she took his hand; "if I ever do anything to make you very, very angry, anything to make you wish me dead, you will remember me as the Florence of your early days,—the Florence who loved you before the world had made her false and heartless."

"Florence, I do not understand."

"Oh, do promise me this," she said in a beseeching voice, "and I will bless you to my dying day,—on my death-bed. But see, there comes Mr. Stockton, and I must dance with him. Your answer quick? Your answer?"

"I think this is our dance, Miss Ruthven; —no. 6, 'a round;'" and the exquisite offered his arm.

Florence smiled and rose. As she was leaving the conservatory she turned round and said in a playful voice, as if she were

speaking of a matter of the most trivial importance, "Well, Leopold, your answer?"

"Should the time come, I promise you;
but may the time never come."

"Thanks," she said in a low tone, "a
thousand times thanks," and she hurried
away with her partner, and was soon mixing
in the dance.

"I cannot understand her," Leopold murmured as he watched his betrothed. "Her
words are as strange as her manner. Pshaw!
I'm mad to have these doubts. She loves
me,—she *must* love me. It would be *too*
cruel were it otherwise. Great Heaven!
how I love her! Forgive her, if she were
false and heartless! Silly child, how could
I be angry with her for anything,—yes, anything?"

He walked away to the other end of the
room, and entered into conversation with
some of the guests to whom he had been
introduced by Edith earlier in the evening.

"When are these fireworks coming off?" said a young man fresh from Trinity, Cambridge.

"At eleven, I think," replied Leopold, looking at his watch; "it is just that hour now."

"I don't seem to care much about fireworks," said the "freshman," trying to look six feet high upon the strength of measuring five-foot-four in his shooting-boots. "Do you?"

"Yes, I like them very well."

"Well, there's no accounting for taste," said the youth with a laugh. "Do you know who that rather nice dark girl over there in the black and yellow dress is? She'd not be bad if she weren't so confoundedly scraggy. Do you know her?"

"Oh yes," replied Leopold, looking calmly down upon his questioner; "it's Miss Ruthven. I am going to marry her sister."

Upon which the "freshman" subsided, and was covered with confusion.

"To be shut up like that!" he muttered indignantly. "Why, a man might just as well be at school!"

At this moment the bell rang for the fireworks, and the drawing-room was deserted for the park.

It was a charming scene. Groups were formed on the green grass of prettily dressed women and black-coated men. Here and there were a few villagers who had gained permission to be present at "the show." There was the sound of laughter, and many a mild flirtation was carried on in the shadow thrown by the trees.

"Surely that shed should be protected," said Leopold, as he passed by the ground sacred to the fireworks. "If a rocket-stick falls on it, it may set the thatch alight."

"It's all right, Guvnor," replied the man

to whom he addressed this remark. "Take greatsh schcare."

From which reply it would seem that the man was drunk.

A few minutes after this, the fireworks began. Very pretty indeed, and very much like other fireworks. The peasantry were greatly impressed, but, to tell the truth, it slightly bored the gentry. There was one amusing incident. The drunken man assisting at the display, to whom Leopold had spoken, in his frantic efforts to be useful if not ornamental, managed to ignite the contents of a large basket of squibs and rockets. The result was a magnificent but unexpected effect. Rockets flew in all directions,—some towards the house, some in the direction of the company. When it was discovered that no harm had been done, there was much laughter at this little *contretemps*.

In the meanwhile a servant from the house had approached Leopold with a letter.

"As the envelope says it's important. Sir," observed the man, "I thought as how I had better bring it to you at once."

Leopold took the note and opened it; it ran as follows :—

" MY DEAR SIR,

" *Pardon me for troubling you, and forgive me for breaking in upon your privacy. If you take my advice, you will keep a sharp look-out upon Mr. Frederick Holston. I have good reasons for believing that he is engaged upon a work calculated to destroy your peace of mind for ever. If I were not sure of what I write, this note would be an impertinence.*

" *Yours sincerely,*

" JOHN DUTTON, *Priest.*"

Leopold stood quite still after reading this letter, and then there came a shout, which grew louder and louder and louder.

"Fire! Fire! Fire!"

CHAPTER X.

"FALSE AS WATER!"

WE must now return to Florence Ruthven,
and follow her history on this eventful evening. It will be remembered that she left
Leopold to waltz with one of her uncle's
guests. The dance over, she excused herself to her partner and left the saloon.

Like one frightened of her own shadow,
she crept up the stairs to her own room.
As she opened the door the moonlight
streamed in through the window, and the
sound of the bell summoning the guests to
the fireworks was heard.

"The time has come at last," she murmured, and trembled. "Great Heaven, what am I doing! But it is too late to think of it now."

She ran to the mantelpiece and struck a light; then she opened her desk and began to write. With a trembling hand she traced the following lines:—

"Forgive me. When you read this I shall be far away. I am not worthy of you, and my love was a mockery. Forgive me and forget me.

"FLORENCE RUTHVEN."

She hurriedly encased the sheet of paper in a directed envelope, and was about to open her wardrobe when a knock at the door startled her.

"Who's there?" she cried, and she hurriedly put the letter in her bosom.

"Only me, Miss," replied the voice of a female outside.

"Come in. Well, Laura, what do you want?"

"Oh, Miss, aren't you coming to see the fireworks? they are so beautiful."

"No, Laura, I have a headache and shall rest for a while; but you can go if you like."

"Oh, thanks, Miss. I shall be so glad," and the delighted servant-maid ran off.

Florence hurriedly opened the wardrobe, and selecting a travelling-cloak, threw it over her ball dress. As she did this there was a brilliant explosion and a loud report, then a dead silence, followed in a moment's time by a shout of merry laughter.

"Poor Leopold!" she said, as she packed up in a small parcel a few of her things. "Poor Leopold, how he will miss me!"

As she said this, she heard a murmur, and a stifling smell of smoke invaded her room. She rushed to the window and looked out,—the shed was on fire, and the flames threw a lurid glare upon the faces of the company. "I can't go yet," she cried; "I shall be discovered if I do."

And she stood by the window looking out upon the flames. By-and-by there was the sound of a loud crackling behind her, and volumes of smoke made their way through the cracks in the door. She rushed to the entrance and threw the portal wide open. She shrank back in terror.

The staircase was on fire!

With her hair down her back, her dress in disorder, and her eyes starting out of her head, she rushed to the window and opened it.

"Help! help!" she screamed, in an agony of fright.

There was a shout when she was recognized, and a babel of voices arose. Directions were tendered from a hundred throats at once. Then she remembered that a ladder led from the top landing on to the roof, and that she might, perhaps, find safety there.

With terror-winged eagerness she sprang to the door and made her way to the landing. The staircase was still burning, but the flames had not as yet reached the upper story. Pale as a ghost, the girl sprang up the stairs and found the ladder. Almost stifled with smoke, and trembling with fright, she climbed towards the roof and reached the leads.

As she did this, a man who had heard the tidings of her incarceration rushed into the house. Regardless of the flames and smoke, he crawled up the burning staircase, which shook and bent beneath his weight. As he reached her room he caught sight of her retreating figure. He rushed up the remaining stairs, and soon joined her on the roof.

As he did this, there was a shout from below, and heaven's sky was lighted up with lurid flames.

"Florence!" he cried, "Florence, my love, I have come to save you!"

She uttered a piercing scream as she recognized him, and a letter dropped from her bosom. He took it up, and showed it to her.

"For God's sake do not read it, Leopold!"

"It is addressed to me, Florence," he said, and opened it.

Then by the light of the fast-encroaching flames he read the letter that Florence had written to him half an hour before.

"I will save your life, my poor girl," he said calmly, but with lips that trembled and hands that shook; "but you have killed my heart for ever!"

The flames reached the ladder as he spoke to her.

End of Book III.

The Story.

BOOK IV.—NEMESIS!

CHAPTER I.

EXTRACTS FROM MISS RUTHVEN'S DIARY.

AT STELSTEAD, *October 1st*, 18——.—Last night seems to me like a dreadful, terrible dream. The fire—the smoke still dances before my eyes,—I can scarcely think—I can only pray. Pray, and earnestly too, thanking God for our great deliverance.

Yes, as I write we are safe—quite safe. I can see through the window the village-road, and there beyond the trees is the curling cord of smoke, telling of the still smouldering ruins of Ruthven Hall. Now that I am comparatively calm, let me write down

the events of last night, as well as I can remember them.

When the outhouse caught fire, I was
standing near Leopold. The flames spread
rapidly, and before the villagers could fetch
the parish engine to our assistance, the dear
old Hall was burning. It was a sad, sad
sight, but we knew not at first how sad.

As I gazed at the burning house, I saw
what seemed to me to be the shadow of a
woman thrown upon the blind of one of the
windows. I could not be sure, for the glare
of the burning outhouse rendered everything within the Hall dark and indistinct.
But the very suspicion that any living being
should be resting in the doomed house was
terrible to bear. I called Leopold, who had
been assisting to extinguish the fire, to come
near me, and pointed out the shadow to
him.

"Have no fear, Edith," he said to me;
"providentially the house is empty,—even

the servants have left it to look at the fireworks. We may save the place yet, if we
only can get the engine in time."

And he hurried away to give some directions to a number of men who were carrying buckets of water. Still I could not
take my eyes away from the window and its
shadow. Indistinct and motionless as it
seemed, it had a terrible fascination, and I
gazed with a feeling of horror and apprehension. After a while my worst fears were
realized. The shadow disappeared, and then
I was certain it belonged to a living being.
I called Leopold a second time to me, and
again expressed my fears. He was about
to answer me when the window I had
watched was thrown violently open, and a
strange unearthly voice—the voice of a woman in mortal terror screamed for help. I
was too far away to recognize the figure,
shrouded as it was in a long cloak, and the
sound of the voice was so unearthly, so

dreadful in its despair that it was impossible to recognize its tones.

"Great God!" cried Leopold, and rushed away to the door of the burning house.

I watched him, and stretched forth my hands, and tried to speak, but could not utter a word. My heart stopped beating as I saw him entering the burning portals. As he came to the door the figure of a man rushed forward. Leopold turned round, snatched up a rope that lay on the ground, and laughed in bitter derision as the new-comer stopped short, fearful of the encroaching flames. Only for a moment heard I this laugh, for then Leopold had rushed into the house, and was lost to my sight. Then I raised my eyes to the window—it was empty!

"She has gained the roof," I heard shouted by a score of voices; and then I saw the cloaked figure far above me. Safe, for the moment, from the fast advancing flames.

It seemed like a frightful vision. I had not the power of motion—speech. I could only gaze on in voiceless terror.

Soon—very soon—Leopold was on the roof too, and then the cloaked figure dropped to the ground behind the balustrade. The poor creature had fainted.

The people near me shouted a number of directions, but Leopold regarded them not. He looked about him, and, seeing a stack of chimneys, attached the rope he carried with him to a part of the brickwork. He tested its strength, and then disappeared for a moment behind the balustrade.

I leant for support against a tree, and could scarcely breathe, for now I saw him bearing the cloaked figure in his arms, and preparing to descend.

A thrill of terror passed through the staring, horror-stricken crowd as he laid hold of the rope and swung in the air. Only a thin cord between two lives and eternity! As I think of it now, I lay down my pen, and try to shut out the fearful sight from my eyes. That moment, that dreadful moment, will haunt me for ever!

The rope slipped a foot, and then became taut. Slowly, surely and steadily Leopold descended in the dead silence of the spectators, and the fearful crackling of the flames. Of all who were there, he only was calm, he only was collected. In a shorter time than it takes me to write these few words, he had reached the ground, and was saved!

I raised my eyes to heaven, and poured out my very soul in praise and thanksgiving. There was a dead silence as he reached the earth, and then there was a loud, a joyous, an exultant shout.

"Edith," I heard him say a moment after; "Edith."

"Thank God you are saved," I cried, and tried to seize his hand in the ecstasy of my joy. But his face repelled me; it was so full of pain and despair—so white—so hopeless, oh, so hopeless!

"Don't try to speak to me, Edith," he said, and his lips trembled; "I cannot bear it! Look to her." And he gave into my arms the cloaked figure, sighed heavily, and was gone.

Scarcely conscious of my burden, I watched him as he hurried away, out into the darkness, with his head resting on his breast, with his trembling hands raised before his eyes—watched him with a feeling of terror and compassion at my heart—watched him until my soul yearned after him, and I was nearly dead with sorrow.

By-and-by, I heard a sigh, and listened to a faint voice. I looked down at the face resting on my bosom, and found in the cloaked figure I clasped in my arms the form of my sister Florence!

"Hide me from him," she cried; "I cannot bear his sight. Oh, hide me from him —oh, *do* hide me from him."

And then she fainted once more, and her cold cheek rested on my bosom.

As we stood thus clasped in one another's arms, some of the ballroom guests came to us, and spoke to me—I know not what. I next remember being lifted into a carriage, and driven away.

This morning, I woke here. I found that we had been brought to Samson's, the cobbler's, house. Our landlord is full of apologies for the poverty of his abode. Superfluous explanations, in my opinion, for the rooms are kept both clean and neat. I am sure I shall regret leaving. We go to-day to Sir John Elliott's place on a visit.

I have seen Florence this morning, but she keeps a rigid silence about the doings of last night. Poor girl! she is sad and pale. Uncle Ralph is here, too; he is ill.

This spot is very lonely. Leopold has not been here to-day. Strange, after—

I must stop at this point. Samson has

just entered the room, and wants to speak to me. From experience I know that it would be useless to attempt to write any longer with him in the room, so I lay down my pen with the intention of resuming it at a more convenient season.

*   *   *   *   *   *

London, November 15*th,* 18——.—I have not had the heart to open this book since my last entry in it until to-day. I have dreaded to write what my pen is now about to record.

Samson came into the room to tell me that Leopold wished to see me. The old man looked very sad as he gave me this message.

"He's terribly changed, Miss," said he, "terribly changed! He's more like a ghost than a human being."

Then he went out, and Leopold opened the door and stood before me. Poor fellow! it pained me to the heart to see him so sad and hopeless.

"Edith," he said in a cold calm voice, "I have come to bid you adieu,—perhaps for ever."

I started back, and I know the colour left my cheeks. I tried to murmur something but could find no words.

"It is better that it should be so," he continued, "much better. Perhaps away from England,—in foreign lands I may learn to forget the past."

"Leave England!" I cried at last, "leave England, home, and—"

"Don't mention her name, Edith," he said, interrupting me, "I must never hear her name again. She is dead to me for ever. You understand, for ever!"

I looked at him in sorrowful surprise.

"You would know what has worked this change? Read this and it will explain my meaning."

He gave me a letter—a shameful cruel letter; a letter that made me blush with indignation, that filled me with shame when I remembered that it was written by my sister.

"Now you know all," he said, and approached the fire. "Let the past be the past," and he thrust the letter in the flames and sighed. "All is over,—over for ever!"

The tears gathered in my eyes and I tried to speak.

"It is better as it is, Edith,—you once told me that she never loved me—you were right. Great God, you were right!" and his frame was shaken by a hysterical sob,— I could not bear to look upon him in his agony.

He soon regained his composure and talked calmly of the future. He discussed with me his plans—he was to go to Africa —to India—anywhere to be away, far away from her. In spite of his *sang froid* I could see how he was suffering,—how dearly he paid for every word.

At last he rose to take his leave. He clasped my hand and said, "Edith, dear Edith, this is the last time, perhaps, that we may meet on earth. I thank you for your kindness—your great, great kindness. You have been my friend—my sister. But it was not to be, dear, it was not to be!"

I thrilled as his hand touched mine. And she had cast him away from her like a worthless toy!

"I shall never forget you, dear sister, Good-bye." He hesitated for a moment, and then said with an effort, "Tell her, Edith—when I have gone—that I forgive her,—that from my heart I forgive her!"

He kissed my forehead, and I saw him no more.

*   *   *   *   *   *

At Stelstead, May 15*th,* 18—.—Back once more in Stelstead, but how different the place seems! This new house, so fresh and cold and staring, cannot compare for a mo-

ment with the dear old Hall. Since Leopold
left England I have only once heard of him.
The Darewood girls met him at Rome last
winter. They said he was looking very ill,
and seemed much annoyed at being recognized. He left the next day. Poor fellow,
how my heart yearns after him!

Florence is staying in London at Lady
Abbott's. From what I hear she seems to
be the belle of the season. Ah! I am well
satisfied to remain here tending on poor
Uncle Ralph, who is sinking, I fear,—he
scarcely ever speaks now; he seems to be
weighed down by some terrible secret.
More than once he has commenced to reveal
to me the story of his trouble, but he has
always broken off at a certain point, leaving
me in ignorance of his secret.

We are to have a visitor here,—no less a
personage than Mr. Holston. I cannot imagine what brings him from London at this
time of the year,—in the very height of the

season. He is no favourite of mine. I
shall be glad when he leaves us.

A less desponding letter from Florence
this morning; the gaieties of town seem to
be consoling her! And to think that *he*
should break his heart about her! Fickle
as water—unstable as sand. I have thought
lately,—is it wicked to hope?

Hope! What hope have I? Poor fool
that I am. I try to dupe myself. Hope!

*   *   *   *   *   *

At Stelstead, June 18*th*, 18—.—I now
understand the reason of Mr. Holston's
visit. From the moment of his arrival he
has seemed to exercise a marvellous influ-
ence over Uncle Ralph. The first morning
he was closeted with my uncle for a couple
of hours. As I passed the library door I
heard loud voices within; a little later, when
I met my uncle, he seemed to be suffering
from great agitation.

He leaves us to-morrow, and last night

Uncle Ralph told me the object of his visit. He is going to marry Florence!

Uncle Ralph has given his consent (reluctantly, I think), and the news has been sent to the 'Court Journal.'

I find that Uncle Ralph has made no attempt to secure Florence's fortune on herself. When I pointed out that Mr. Holston did not enjoy a spotless reputation, my uncle became angry, and declared that Mr. Holston was honest, chivalrous,—in fact, a gentleman. In spite of this, I am sure my uncle hates him. Mr. Holston has his way in everything. He is all in all here; no one seems brave enough to thwart him.

No, not "no one;" for there is an exception. Father Dutton has seen my uncle several times, and has urged him to beware of Mr. Holston. Without effect. My relative seems infatuated.

"I am afraid, Miss Ruthven," said Father Dutton to me this morning; "I am afraid

that Holston knows some terrible secret,—
holds your uncle in his power."

Can the priest be right?

*   *   *   *   *   *

London, October 25th, 18—.—The marriage is over; Florence is Frederick Holston's wife.

And this is the end of Leopold's dream!
It may be that it is better as it is. Florence
came to my room last night in tears, and
told me she was miserable.

" I don't know what I am doing," she
sobbed out.

" Do you mean to say that you don't care
for Frederick Holston?" I asked.

" I don't know," she replied. " I fear
him—he terrifies me. I *must* marry him!"

It was painful to watch her distress. For
the first time since *his* absence my heart
warmed towards her.

" My sister," I said, taking her in my

arms; "my sister, we have been separated for a long, long while. This should not be, dear; this must not be."

"I am sure it hasn't been my fault, Edith. Ever since Leopold left so hurriedly, so cruelly, you have not been the same person."

"Hurriedly—cruelly! Had Leopold no cause to go?"

"Oh, yes; of course he had. I have been very wicked and miserable, and everybody hates me; but he might have stayed, he must have known that I could never forget his rescuing me on that dreadful night—never, never, never!"

"What, do you mean to say that you still love him?"

"I don't know," she said, bursting into tears; "I only know that I am very, very miserable!"

"This marriage ought not to take place, Florence."

"It must, Edith; it must. I dare not —
you hear—I dare not refuse him!"

And now they are married. Heaven help
her, poor child; Heaven help us all. Not a
word has been heard about him. He is still
abroad. Will he never return? And if he
does return, what then? Oh, how my poor
hope dies within me as I think of him!

CHAPTER II.

A MEETING AT WIESBADEN.

WIESBADEN in the season is a charming and
instructive place. Hospitable to a degree
are the town authorities; fine, indeed, are
the first-class hotels. But more hospitable
and still finer than burghers and hosts are
the bankers of the Kursaal, who welcome
the coming guest, and weep (metaphorically)
over those who depart from them. The rich
traveller is made quite at home in the splendid rooms of the Kursaal,—he is fêted and
played to, furnished with reading-rooms,
drawing-rooms, dining-rooms; he is asked

to concerts and invited to balls,—it is impossible to make too much of him. So careful are his friends of his comfort that they actually provide him with the means of winning a little extra money to add to his hoard by taking his chance at the tables. So he feasts and dances, and listens to the music and plays, and leaves nothing more valuable to his hospitable hosts as a memento of his visit than his gold! And yet there are those who saw that Wiesbaden is an expensive place, and that the Kursaal, with all its comforts, is nothing better than a snare and a delusion.

Two years after the date of our last extract from Miss Ruthven's diary, Wiesbaden was at the height of its popularity. The military band played in the gardens, with its trees and lake and fountain, and thousands listened to the music. Lively Frenchwomen were there in all the frippery of fashion, perfectly neat, but extremely ill-favoured,—

with dresses fit for Beauty to wear, and faces exactly suited for marriage with the Beast. There were German girls, blonde and fat, with light blue eyes and substantial busts,—girls who would sooner or later emulate their mothers in ugliness and weight. Then there were *blasées* maidens from England, who, after having "done" one season at home, had come across the sea to "do" another one abroad. Then there were *petits crevés* from Paris, in gorgeous apparel, and *pince nez*,—with coats that were fully as ill-made as—as their trousers and waistcoats! Then there were Englishmen of the best class,—in other words, gentlemen, quiet, neatly dressed, and reserved, who regarded with some surprise and slight amusement the strange "get-ups" of the French juveniles. Then there were Prussian officers in full uniform, with lots of sword and a deal of moustaches, who lounged about the place like favoured footmen,—knowing no one

and recognized by none. And the cosmo-
politan crowd promenaded up and down,
listening to the music and criticizing one
another. The sight would have rejoiced the
heart of an artist,—there was so much paint;
would have delighted the nose of a soldier,
—there was so much powder! And the
band played its sweet waltzes, drowning
the voices of the croupiers as they plied
their monotonous trade in the rooms hard
by, and absolutely overwhelming the sharp
" whirr" of the roulette-ball.

At one of the little tables outside the
Kursaal sat an Englishman listening to the
music and sipping some coffee. He was not
an old man, in spite of his white hair and
bronzed complexion, and certainly could not
have told more years than thirty. His face
was marked with deep lines caused by much
sorrow,—sorrow long gone by, for now his
expression denoted resignation and perfect
calm. He gazed carelessly at the prome-

naders as they passed by, and lighted a cigar. As he sat thus, another Englishman lounged up to the very spot, and called one of the waiters up to him.

He was a dissipated-looking young man, this Englishman, with bloodshot eyes and bleared features, and unsteady gait. He was rather "loudly" dressed, and seemed to have contracted a "horsey swagger," smacking of Newmarket stables and "corner bad form." People looking at him closely would have imagined him to be a gentleman gone to the bad. And so he was. Fat and podgy, with a complexion of brick-red and cheese-white, telling of strong drink and late hours, he was scarcely the man one would have put up for one's pet club, or introduced to one's own people.

" Here, you fellow," said this unprepossessing-looking person when the waiter approached; " do you speak English ?"

" Yes, sare,—very well,—you take rosbif?"

" Hang ' rosbif.' "

" Yes, sare,—you not take it?   Ah, then, you take de bifteck?"

" Hang equally ' bifteck.'   How comes it that an Englishman can't move a step on the Continent without being pestered with bifteck and rosbif?   We never think of eating the abominations at home.   No, what I want is some brandy."

" Yes, sare," and the waiter prepared to move away.

" Stay a moment; look here, do you speak French?"

" Oui, Monsieur."

" Eh bien, parlez-vous Français au lieu d'Anglais, parce que votre Anglais n'est pas bon,—c'est impossible pour votre Français d'être plus mauvais que votre Anglais.   You understand,—now get off, and look sharp back."

The abashed waiter grinned uncomfortably, and hurried away.

The Englishman to whom the reader was introduced some pages back regarded his compatriot with a feeling of something much akin to disgust. He looked at him languidly, as he would have watched the uncouth gestures of some monkey at the Zoological Gardens for a few minutes, and then his careless stare deepened into a gaze of genuine astonishment.

"It surely cannot be—so changed," he murmured; and, as he noticed that the waiter had returned with the brandy, he listened attentively to catch the tones of the stranger's voice.

"V'là, M'sieur, v'là eau de vie—un p'tit tasse!" exclaimed the Kellner with a flourish, and he placed a small glass bottle (holding about half a pint of brandy) and a liqueur glass on the table.

"Stick to English," was the reply of the traveller; "bad as it is, I think it's rather better than your French! And here, I say, what's this? Get me a tumbler."

The waiter stared a little, and replaced the liqueur glass as directed with a tumbler.

" Ah, that's better; got change for a five-thaler note? Take for the whole, I shall finish it."

The waiter stared once more, gave the required change, and hurried off, mumbling something to himself (in German) about the drinking capabilities of " Milors" the English.

" I was not mistaken,—poor girl! poor girl!" murmured the grave man seated at the other table; " what a fate!"

The dissipated Englishman coolly poured the contents of the glass bottle into his tumbler, and drank it off with as little compunction and effort as an ordinary man would have partaken of pure water.

" That's good," said he, smacking his lips. " Great institution, brandy; it puts life into a fellow. And now that I have pulled myself together again, I will go back to the table, and see how *she* is getting on."

He rose from his chair, and, with rather
an unsteady step, walked towards the door
leading to the gaming-rooms of the Kursaal.
The other Englishman, who had not lifted
his eyes from him since he had heard him
speak to the waiter, rose too, and followed
him at a distance. Thus, they walked towards the same hell,—one with the swagger
of drunken desperation, the other with the
cautious step of deadly hate; one noisy and
overbearing, the other silent and stealthy,
and both hopeless.

The first made his way rudely through the
throng of idlers, looking about him from
right to left with defiant glances as he met
the gaze of those who had known him once
and now knew him no longer; the second
with his eyes fixed steadily upon the man
walking before him, without thought or
sight for those who hemmed him round
about. And as the two enemies (for they
were bitter enemies) walked thus, follower

and followed, the military band played its
gayest tunes, and the world of Wiesbaden
chattered and flirted and laughed, as if
" vengeance" were an idle word, and " re-
venge" a sound meaning absolutely nothing.

The first Englishman entered the ball-
room of the Kursaal, and was about to pro-
ceed into the inner apartments, when the
doorkeeper (who, being a lackey, was, of
course—the spot being Germany—costumed
like a field-marshal, in sword and epaulettes,
and silver and gold) opposed his entrance.

" What do you mean?" cried the young
man. " Have I not lost thousands at these
confounded tables ? Is not that a sufficient
passport—eh, you rogue, eh ?"

" Sare, I fear, is not well," said the gorgeous doorkeeper, civilly but firmly. " Sare
will come to-morrow, when he is well; then
he will go in."

" Hang to-morrow. I tell you I *will* go

in,—d'ye hear? Do you want me to make a disturbance, and cry out my losses? Eh, is that your game, you confounded thief?" and the Englishman pushed rudely past.

The doorkeeper beckoned to a quiet-looking man, dressed in black, and gave him some direction. The quiet-looking man nodded, and followed the unwelcome "guest" into the gaming-rooms.

While this was going on, the second Englishman waited in the ball-room, and when he presented himself at the door was passed in without comment. On entering, he found a large crowd of people, standing thickly round the tables, watching the roulette-balls and the cards; but the other Englishman he could see nowhere—he had gone.

Yes; he had gone into another room, where the play was higher and the gambling more desperate. He had gone to form one of a group standing round the table, with its green cloth and white figures, with its ever-rolling ball and its monotonous-voiced, impassible croupier, with its heaps of gold and rolls of silver, with its votaries and its victims.

A terrible scene—often painted, and never painted too strongly—often cursed, and never cursed too deeply. Stupid to a degree in its stolid, skilless work,—fatal to a degree in its ceaseless, hungry greed for gain. Who can refrain from condemning it? Who has not condemned it, with a heart and soul fitting a man made in the image of the Great Creator? And shall I add my faltering testimony to the overwhelming evidence, branding the fatal table as fit only for the fare of the Devil—the banquets of Hell; shall I wend my wavering steps in the path trodden by great thinkers and eloquent authors; shall I lift the sword wielded so often by mightier soldiers than I; shall I hold the lance so often guided by greater champions than it will ever be my fate even to squire? It seems presumptuous, and yet it shall be done.

The Englishman took ·his place at the table, and looked around him as if in search of some one he knew. His eyes rested first upon a poor old lady, who watched the roulette as it whirled round with breathless anxiety. She sighed as she lost, and her hand trembled as she pushed another thaler from her poor little heap on to a number, and then waited once more for the sharp " whirr " of the ivory ball—so small and yet so fatal—to tell her if she had won a new dress, to replace the threadbare robe she wore, or had lost—a dinner ! As he watched her, a pale-faced girl came up to her, and seemed to implore her to come away, and then the old woman with tearful eyes and trembling voice recounted her loss, and ex- plained the reason of her bad luck. And even while she spoke, the greedy ball had robbed her of her paltry coin, and she eagerly reached forward to stake another thaler on the *rouge!* Next his eyes rested upon a beautiful woman dressed in white silk, and wearing jewelled rings on her fingers, and costly lockets on her cold passionless bosom, who swept her gold towards the figure that last had won, and waited calmly, almost scornfully for the voice of the croupier to declare the next winning number. She lost, and another heap of gold was pushed by the rake she held in her hand to the spot she fancied, and then she waited once more for the monotonous voice of the croupier. Calm as the waveless sea on the surface, a very tempest of wild emotions were holding their revels in her heart; and she played on as she had played for hours gone by—as she would play for hours to come. Then he looked at a young girl scarcely eighteen, with flushed cheeks and eyes unnaturally bright, who trembled with fierce excitement as she won, who glared like a wild beast when she lost, who was no longer sane in the ecstasy or despair of the moment, who had heart, thought, soul only for the ever-moving ivory ball,—ears, brain, understanding only for the monotonous voice of the croupier. Then one of his countrymen attracted his notice. A young Englishman, drawn to the table by lack of employment or want of amusement, was playing with great zeal and zest. He was winning largely, and as he played, the woman in the white dress turned her cold passionless eyes towards him, and backed his luck as she would have backed the chance of a race-horse, or staked her money in the city. And opposite the Englishman was a desperate German, who had won largely (like the Englishman facing him) yesterday, and who was pale, cold, and ruined to-day ! And round about these figures were abandoned women and dishonoured men, princes and sharpers, maidens and leaders of the *demi-monde*, ladies and brutes, elbowing one another, pushing one another in the great equality of the search after gold—the unhallowed republic of Mammon!

At last our Englishman recognized the person of whom he was in search. She was a poor flaxen-haired, pale-faced girl, who played listlessly, with tears in her blue eyes and with many a sigh that shook her fragile frame as the earthquake shakes the trembling village, as the avalanche sweeps away the puny hamlet that bars its progress. But what cared the excited crowd for her emotion? Was not the roulette-ball there to attract their attention away from her tears; was not the loud military band playing its gayest tunes, to drown her sighs and those who sighed round about her?

Our Englishman approached this poor feeble player, and, shaking her roughly by the arm, leant over her and whispered something in her ear. She trembled as she listened to his voice, and, gathering her shawl round her, rose from the table and followed the man as he walked unsteadily in front of her from the room. They passed among the crowd of the players towards the gardens of the Kursaal. As they left the ball-room, the music of the military band (which had sounded until now subdued) broke out with its brazen clamour and echoing drums, as if in triumph of the ruin reigning within.

The man led the way to a secluded part of the gardens, threw himself on a seat, and, looking fiercely into her pale, patient face, cried out sharply,—

" Well ?"

She trembled before him, and putting her poor thin fingers before her eyes, began to cry.

" None of this nonsense," he said brutally. " What have you done ? How much have

you won ?   Here, give me your purse,—let
me see for myself !"

She stretched out her trembling hand and
gave him her *porte-monnaie.*

" What !" he almost screamed out as he
examined the purse. " Empty !   Empty !
Empty !"

" I couldn't help it," she cried. " I couldn't
help it,—the luck went against us.   The
rouge turned up thirteen times running
indeed, indeed, I couldn't help it !"

He stared away from her hopelessly and
savagely, and ground his teeth, and cursed
her as she stood before him.   At last he
turned round and, fixing his bloodshot eyes
upon her, cried out,—

" Do you know what you have done, my
lady, in losing that twenty-five thaler note ?
Why we are penniless now.   Do you hear ?
—we are ruined !"

" Oh, surely not that !" she cried, wringing her hands.   " My fortune—"

"*Your* fortune!" he cried scornfully. "*Your* fortune, my lady, has gone,—every penny of it. It just covered the settling for the Leger. No, we have not a penny,—not a d—d penny!"

"But wouldn't your father—"

"My father!—curse my father! You know he has turned his back upon me ever since I was kicked out of the Hamilton for that beastly card affair. No, there's no hope, —I tell you no hope!"

"Don't say that, dear," she said, and she timidly approached him, and with all a woman's tenderness tried to wind her arm about his neck.

"Don't touch me!" he cried. "Why it was you who lost our last thaler, you—you milk-faced bag o' bones,—you—you--"

And he cast her brutally from him, and called her a name that brought the red blood into her poor pale cheeks, and made her weary eyes swim with tears.

"Oh, Leopold, Leopold!" she cried, and turned from him.

"What's that you are calling out?" he almost screamed. "What's that, you — you light o' love?"

And he rose unsteadily from the bench and strode towards her.

"Frederick Holston!" she sobbed out, "may God forgive you, for I never can!"

The poltroon—the miserable, drunken poltroon—struck at her! The poor girl gave a faint scream as the blow fell upon the weak arm raised to guard her head, and then cried—

"You coward,—you base, wicked coward!"

And then, turning from him with heaving bosom and tearful eyes, she disappeared behind the bushes, leaving him alone.

He stared about him like a man in a dream, and then sank back upon the bench.

"What have I done!" he exclaimed at last. "Great Heavens, what have I done!"

He sat thus for ten minutes, regardless of the crushing of the gravel, telling of the near approach of another promenader. So absent was he that the new-comer had time to get up close to him before he took any notice of his presence. Even when the man stood before him he did not recognize him.

The fresh arrival was none other than the Englishman with the white hair, who had followed him so closely before he entered the gambling-rooms.

"Good evening, Mr. Holston."

"What, you know me!" cried Freddy, half in joy, half with suspicion.

"Perfectly. The last time we met was at the burning of Ruthven House."

"What! then you are Richard Harwood?"

"Or Leopold Lawson, whichever you please. The last time you met me under that name, you helped to hang my father.

I am here now to pay the obligation. Can I do anything for you?"

He said this coldly and cruelly. Freddy stared at him with surprise and horror; then he murmured in a weak, trembling voice,—

"Don't hit a man when he's down. I am ill and starving; and—and—" And his lips trembled, and the tears gathered in his eyes.

"Come, come," said Leopold in a softer voice, "I owe you no love, as you know well enough; but you are not the *great* culprit. Come, cheer up; I may be able to help you. But, first, how is your wife?"

He tried to ask this question firmly and carelessly, but, in spite of all his efforts, his voice trembled a little as he uttered the words.

Freddy noticed the tremor, and rejoiced at finding out an unhealed wound in his enemy's heart. He did not allow Leopold to notice his exultation, however, and only replied,—

" She's as well as can be expected, poor girl ! We have had a hard life lately—a very hard life !"

" Where is she now ? I ask you because I have no wish to meet her. It might be painful for her."

"Oh," said Freddy with a smile of gratified hate as he listened to the falter in Leopold's voice. " She is staying to-day with some ladies of her acquaintance. If you *really* wish it, I will take care that we don't run across her."

" If I *really* wish it; what do you mean ?"

" Nothing," replied Freddy with a ghost of his old laugh, and with a stealthy side-glance, " if *you* mean nothing. I only re-membered that I am deuced poor and you are deuced rich. That was all."

" Well ?"

" Well—Florence was an old flame of yours, and—"

" Well ?"

"Oh, nothing," said Freddy, seeing something dangerous in the other's eye; "nothing,—how fiery you are! But there, let's change the subject."

"Willingly. Are you engaged this evening?"

"No," said Freddy with a cynical laugh. "Since I have been out at elbows my cards have fallen off terribly. I am considered *gauche*,—you know it is so horribly old-fashioned to starve!"

"Come, then, we will have a little dinner at my hotel, and over our wine you shall tell me your troubles, and then I will see what can be done."

Leopold shuddered with disgust as Freddy linked his arm within his own, but regained his usual composure as he thought, "It is for her sake I do all this,—for her sake, poor girl!"

CHAPTER III.

THE HOLLOW TRUCE.

IT was nine o'clock in the evening. Most of the world at Wiesbaden had dined, and were returning to the Kursaal to listen to the concert given in the ball-room by the Prussian Military Band (which band, musically speaking, seemed to have a hard time of it), and to throng round the tables either as players or as spectators. The town itself was quiet enough,—the silence of the streets being broken only by the rumbling of a carriage over the stones, or by the sharp whistle of the engine, telling of a train's departure either for Bingen or Mayence. Leopold and his guest sat over their coffee. During dinner the conversation had not been very lively, or very well-sustained. Leopold was moody, and Freddy had lost all his usual vivacity. Their freedom of speech, too, was curtailed somewhat by the presence of the waiter, who spoke English, of course, as well as his native German. When the attendant —after a vain attempt to make them drink " pell ale " in liqueur glasses as a *chasse café* (a custom of the English, so he said)—had withdrawn, they began to breathe more comfortably.

" Well, Holston," said Leopold, lighting a cigar, " come tell me what's the matter with you. But first you are sure your wife is with her friends,—you will not be keeping her up ?"

"Oh, no ; she's all right. She won't be in till eleven. The people she's with always go to the Kursaal in the evening ; besides,

I told her before she left me that I should
dine by myself to night, as I felt so slow.
Oh, no; she's all right."

"Very well then, take a cigar, and tell
me what is the matter."

"What is the matter?" replied Freddy
with a bitter laugh. "Egad, it would be
easier to tell you what is not the matter.
Why, Sir, within two years I have lost every
penny I had in the world,—every penny,
Sir!"

"Well," said Leopold, looking at the end
of his cigar, and puffing a cloud of smoke;
"but you received a fortune with—with—"

"Florence?" put in Freddy, and he noticed that his *quasi* rival winced at the name.
"But what of that? It went in a very few
months."

"And did you settle nothing on your
wife,—was nothing ever settled upon her?"

"Nothing."

Leopold pushed away his chair in disgust,

and turned away his head from his guest. Freddy, noticing these gestures of disapproval, hastened to defend himself.

"Look here, Harwood or Lawson (choose the name you like best from the two I offer you), look here. When we last discussed monetary matters, I told you I regarded marriage as only the means to an end. Gold, and lots of it, was the only metal that would gild properly that bitterest of pills—a wife. Those were my sentiments as a bachelor; as a husband they have undergone no alteration,—on the contrary, they have been fully confirmed."

"Well?"

"Well, I am afraid there's very little sentiment in my composition. I don't mind telling such an old friend as you that I married for money." Leopold winced. "Yes, it's too true. I saw, I married, I spent it! And now, by a series of cruel reverses, I am reduced to my last penny. Why, the very dinner I have just eaten has been as welcome to me as if it had been given to me in charity! I am a pauper, a poor beggar,—an utterly ruined man!"

And the fellow very nearly began to cry as he regarded the self-painted picture of his woes.

The dining-room was on the ground floor and level with the street. During this conversation, a woman who concealed her face with a shawl had stood in the shadow, gazing intently at Leopold. She was very pale, and the tears gathered in her eyes as she watched him. At this point, however, she was disturbed by Freddy, who rose from the table and approached the window to breathe the fresh air. She was about to hurry off when she was discovered.

"Eh! what's this?" cried Holston. "A listener! Come, stop, my dear,—let me look at your face, to see if it's a pretty one. Come, don't be shy."

She broke from him and fled away. As she disappeared in the darkness his laugh rang in her ears, his words sank deeply in her heart.

"Heaven help me!" she cried at last. "I can bear it no longer! I can bear it no longer!"

And with her face in her hands, and her fragile frame shaken by sobs, she made her way through the forsaken gardens of the Kursaal.

"What was it?" asked Leopold, as Freddy returned to the table.

"Oh, nothing. Only some beggar girl, either listening to our talk or, what is more likely, looking at our dinner. But, there, you shall have the story of all my sorrows and reverses."

And then he began a long story of how he had lost this and that,—how he had been deceived here and betrayed there. He became quite pathetic as he proceeded, and painted himself as a martyr to circumstances, a hero overborne by colossal difficulties. There was meanness in every sentence, a lie in nearly every word. The picture he presented to Leopold was effective, but the pigments he used were rancid and an abomination.

" Are you quite done ?" asked his host at last, when Freddy seemed to have reached the end of his narrative.

" Yes, quite."

" Well, I think it's just as well to be perfectly frank in this matter."

" I agree with you."

" Well, now, Holston, I don't suppose you imagine that I bear you any great love."

" No,—taking all things into consideration, it is possible that you may not."

" Still I am inclined to forget the past. It's years ago now, and you are down in the world, and,—there, I wish to feel friendly towards you, and to regard yesterday and the days before yesterday as if they had never existed."

"Very kind of you," said Freddy, and even now he could not suppress his accustomed sneer.

"Kind or unkind, I intend to stand your friend. You tell me you are penniless?"

"You know the position of my affairs to a nicety."

"Well, I am rich enough to assist you. You shall have a hundred pounds a quarter on these conditions."

"Ah, *now* we come to business. What are the conditions?"

"First, you must pay the money over to your wife, and she must spend it."

"Hum!"

"Secondly, you must never let her suspect that the money comes from me."

"Oh, I don't mind that so much."

"Thirdly, you must get your wife to send

a receipt for the money through you, to an address I will give you; and, lastly, she must address a letter to her unknown friend reporting matters from quarter to quarter."

"Why the last stipulation?"

"Oh, only because I know your fine contempt for women, Holston; I want to be sure that you are kind to—"

He stopped short, looked at the man before him, and murmured, "Poor girl, poor girl!"

"Well," said Freddy, "I see no objection to your plan; on the contrary, I think it very civil of you. Of course you will get it back some day."

"Of course!"

"Any security, I suppose, would be unnecessary with men of honour,—one's word is as good as one's bond?"

"Quite so; your word, doubtless, is quite as good as your bond."

After a little more conversation, and the passing of certain bank-notes, the two young

men gave each other "good night," and
parted. When Freddy had gone, Leopold
sat down by the window, and looked out
into the starlight night

"I have done what I could for the poor
child," he murmured. "To be wedded for
life to that brute—that infernal snob! Poor
girl—poor girl!"

He rose from the chair and closed the
window. Walking into his bedroom, he
lighted the candles, placed them upon the
table, and fetched his desk. He set it down
beside the candles, opened it, and drew a
chair up to the table.

"To think that I should meet her here!
To meet her just as I turn my steps home-
ward to avenge my father's murder—the
murder so long unavenged. The murder I
should have avenged years and years ago.
Sorrow and misfortune—the very wrath of
God—have taught me to accept that legacy
of vengeance left to me by the dead. And

yet when I turn homewards: when I commence the hunt, she bars my progress, as she did before. Ah, there's the rub,—*as she did before!*"

He looked at a bundle of letters written by a female's hand for a few minutes, then pressed them to his lips, and then sealed them up in a sheet of foolscap paper. Then he touched a spring and a secret drawer flew open. He put the packet in the drawer and closed it.

"Adieu for ever?" he cried, when he had done this. "And now for work. I must leave here to-morrow for Cologne, then to Paris, and then to London. When I am there, I must find out Barman. And after that Sir Ralph Ruthven must beware —no faltering this time. He must prove his innocence or I lead him to death, even as he led my father to the gallows!"

And then he closed his desk, and, kneeling down by his bedside, prayed to his God for guidance and support.

In the meanwhile, Freddy pursued his way towards his lodgings, mumbling as he went incoherent sentences. As he passed by a *café*, he lounged in, and spent some of the change out of his five-thaler note in purchasing some brandy.

After this refreshment his mumbling became indistincter; his words even more incoherent than before. He sang snatches of songs, and stopped every now and then to hold converse with himself.

"Freddy, old f'la," he said, stopping short and rocking on his heels and toes, like a crazy ship in a heavy sea; "Freddy, old f'la, you've done a good stroke o' business, —a very good stroke o' business."

And then he walked on again until he arrived unsteadily at his lodgings. After fumbling at the door for some time with his latch-key, he at last gained admission.

He stumbled upstairs into the sitting-room and lighted a candle. On the table lay two letters—one with the English postmark.

This he took up, leaving the other, which was stampless, untouched. He opened the note he held in his hand, and after some difficulty, began to understand.

"Eh!" he cried out; "old Ruthven won't stump up any more. Soon see about that —very soon see about that."

He took the light, and reeled up to his bedroom. He held the candle over the bed; it was empty.

"She hasn't come in, hasn't she! Very well—very well, I shay, she must get in as she can. I won't wait up for her—not likely. I shay not likely."

And the brute began to undress.

All this while, there was a letter waiting unopened on the table of the sitting-room addressed to Holston, and signed by Florence. If anything *could* have sobered Master Freddy at that moment, it would have been the contents of that neglected, tear-stained letter.

CHAPTER IV.

LAYING THE TRAIN.

IT was a wintry night in November,—the rain and sleet were falling heavily, and the King's Road, Chelsea, was accordingly not particularly inviting in the surrounding gloom. The King's Road, Chelsea, is never a very beautiful place, and in the rain and sleet it simply becomes horrible. Why, scarcely a costermonger, or, to go further, even a French marquis, would have selected it for his home at such a time,—the latter preferring, most probably, the neighbouring Fulham or the water-side Vauxhall to the rain-beaten Chelsea. Trade was not very brisk on the evening in question. Meat went off slowly at the butchers', and boots, and coats and dresses, and warming-pans and family . bibles, were quoted at ridiculously low prices at—the pawnbrokers'!

The weather had had its effect even upon the inhabitants of the unpopular locality,— among the rest upon Mr. John Barman, the detective. This gentleman sat before his fire, in his little parlour, reading a newspaper and smoking a pipe. His face expressed the deepest disgust.

"Call this a picture of an execution?" he cried, regarding the illustrated paper he held in his hand with profound contempt. "Why, it's no more like an execution than this here sketch is like a murder. Why, it's—it's quite ridicklus!" And he threw the paper from him and refilled his pipe. After smoking for a short time he rang the bell, and waited for the appearance of the little servant acting as maid-of-all-work to the landlady.

He had not to wait long; the little woman (a very small child about ten years old) soon put in an appearance and asked him what he wanted.

"What do I want, Maria Susan? What don't I want, Maria Susan?" he said in a pompous voice (*chez lui* he was much given to imitating celebrated "leaders" at the bar by whom he had been professionally examined in the witness box). "Now, take your time—we don't want to fluster you,—but remember what you may say now may be used against you—where is the sugar?

The little servant went to the sideboard, opened it, and reappeared with the sugar basin.

"Now, Maria Susan, be good enough to take that sugar basin in your hand, look at it well, and tell us if it contains the same number of lumps of sugar as it did when I put it back in the cupboard last night?

"Please, I don't know, Sir."

"But you *must* 'know, Sir;' Maria Susan, you *must* know. But there, put it down for the present; we will come to it again by-and-by. Now produce the whisky bottle."

The little servant tremblingly obeyed his orders. "Ah, this is serious—much more serious," said the detective, holding the bottle up to the light, "why, it's nearly half gone! Maria Susan, it is my painful duty to inform you that to pilfering, burglary, arson, and other genteel accomplishments you have now added drinking. You are a drunkard—a swine—Maria Susan, and it's no use for you to attempt to deny it, because it won't do."

The poor little servant forced one of her dirty little fists in her weak little eye, and began to snivel.

"I wouldn't go for to do such a thing, Mr. Barman. I never was 'toxicated in my life."

"This won't do, Maria Susan; why, this very moment I believe you are reeling with drink,—yes, absolutely reeling with drink, or, as the vulgar would put it, 'beastly tight.' Don't dare to contradict me. Don't you know that police constables are the very best judges in the world of intoxication? If you don't, go to the magistrates and hear what *they* say about it."

The little servant snivelled dismally, and complained in deep distress that Mr. Barman was always "at her."

"Yes, I am, Maria Susan, but it is my duty. Now, come, is it not a pity that you, with natural abilities that might have placed you one day on the Judicial Bench, should have fallen so low as to absolutely be accused of sugar-stealing? But there, don't do it again. Now you may cut away."

The little servant quickly profited by the gracious permission, and the detective was once more left alone. He mixed himself a glass of whisky-and-water, and sat smoking before the fire.

"Times are bad," said he, puffing away at his pipe; "very bad. The profession is going to the devil. Scarcely a divorce case to be had anywhere; as for murder, it's quite a drug in the market. What there is of it is vulgar, mere open-day head-smashing! Pshaw! Any fool could do that kind of thing! But the poisoners, the clever manipulators, have all died out,—every one of 'em!"

There was no disputing this fact, as Mr. Calcraft could have told him. He went on smoking and grumbling.

"No, nothing left. The last clever thing I had anything to do with was that Raymond murder. Ah, that was a pleasant affair,—so neat and so very genteel—so very genteel! Ah!"

And he sighed heavily, and smoked on in silence for a few minutes. Then he said,

"I did right about that affair—I know I

did right. It would have been a cruel thing to have let him go on with it, even if he had wished to. Eh, what do you want?"

This question was addressed to the little servant who stood trembling before him.

" Please, Sir, there's a gentleman a-waiting downstairs who says as 'ow 'e wants to see you partickler."

" What's his name?"

" 'Ere's 'is card, Sir;" and the mite held out a piece of cardboard.

" Show him up at once." said the detective. " Talk of the ——. Well, I wonder what brought *him* here."

At this moment Leopold Lawson was ushered into the room. Barman rose to receive him.

" I have taken you by surprise. You didn't expect to see me?"

" I can't say I did, Sir, but you are very welcome; won't you take a seat, Sir? *I* am drinking whisky."

" Thanks very much, Mr. Barman, but I will take no spirits;"—he drew a chair to the fire and continued, " when we last met you were conducting an affair for me which I stopped abruptly. You were surprised at my conduct ?"

" We are never surprised at anything in our profession, Sir; no, you paid me. You were the employer, I the employed. It wasn't for me to say anything."

" Well, Mr. Barman, I have returned to England a different man. I went away feeble, unstable, unreliable. I have returned determined, feelingless, steadfast,—with a purpose that shall be pursued to the bitter end."

The detective glanced at him as he said this. Yes, of a verity he was changed—fearfully changed.

" Now, you naturally want to know why I am here at this hour of the night. I will tell you, because I cannot rest until I have

done my duty.   A curse has rested upon me
for years past, and I *must* remove it.   I
have come to you to-night to help me as
you helped me before."

The detective looked at him in surprise.
His visitor spoke coldly and calmly, but his
syllables fell upon the detective's ear like
the words of doom.

" No," continued Leopold, " you are
wrong.   I am not mad, I am only determined.   But to cut the matter short, I come
to you to-night, Mr. Barman, upon the same
business as before."

" The same business !"

" Yes; I wish once more to sift the Raymond murder to the bottom."

" *You* want to sift it ?"

The detective leant back in his chair, and
regarded his visitor with eyes full of surprise.   He scratched his head, and passed
his hand across his chin thoughtfully.   He
cleared his throat once or twice, and made a

movement as if he would speak, and then relapsed into silence. ,

" Well ?" said Leopold.

" Well, Sir," at last exclaimed Barman, and he looked straight into the fire as he spoke, " of course you know your own business best, but do you think it wise to begin that affair over again after all this while? You see, I considered that there matter done and finished. It ain't my business to offer a suggestion, and it may seem like a liberty, but wouldn't it be better to cut it? That's the point,—wouldn't it be better to cut it?"

And the detective gave a sigh of relief, as if he had performed some difficult act of self-sacrifice, and true nobility.

"You made a very sensible remark just now, Mr. Barman."

" Yes, Sir ?"

" Yes; you said it was not for you to dictate to me, as I was the employer and you the employed."

" Well, Sir, I may have said as much."

" Quite so. Profit by your own words, please,—don't dictate to me. You understand ?"

" Yes, Sir, I understand :" and he murmured in a low tone, " a wilful man must have his own way."

" Perhaps you'd rather give up the business yourself ?"

" Not I, Sir," rejoined the detective quickly. " Why, only just as you came in I was thinking about it, and saying to myself what a pity it was to spoil such a neat affair. Why it's absolutely cruel,—that's what it is. No, Sir; if any one's to do it, let me be the man."

" Well, then, you undertake the task ?"

" Yes, Sir, if you *will* go into it."

" You have heard what I have said."

" Yes, Sir, I have. After all, business is business, all the world over."

" Do your suspicions still point to the same person ?"

"What, Sir Ralph? Yes, Sir; I am more certain than ever."

"Why? Remember your accusation must be supported by the strongest proof, to be pardonable."

"Law bless you, Sir, John Barman knows what he's about. I am always careful in genteel cases. Why I had it from the mouth of young Mr. Holston,—not that we can expect much from him now that he's married the young lady. It wouldn't do, you see, 'cause he's one of the family."

"From the mouth of Frederick Holston!" said Leopold slowly, and, in spite of his cold, grave voice, his lips trembled and his hand shook.

"Law bless you, Sir, he's a sharp 'un, is Mr. Holston. He was cool enough about it. It's a pity he ain't in the profession; he'd be a credit to us."

"What do you mean?"

"Why, Sir, from information I received

it struck me that he might know something about the matter, so I went to his chambers in London. I saw him, Sir, and then he gave me a valuable link in the chain of evidence. At least, not gave it me, but let me have a look at it."

"A link in the chain of evidence?"

"Yes, Sir, and a very good one it was. On the night of Raymond's murder he saw Lady Ruthven a-altering the hall-clock. 'Well,' says I, 'that is a good thing! You'll swear to it of course, Sir!'—'Swear to it!' says he: 'not I. And you just take my advice, Mr. Barman, don't you go any further in this here case. It's no business of yours, and, mark my words, you'll make a mess of it.' With that he bows me out. I dare say you've heard, Sir, that he married the baronet's niece within a year of the time I met him. Oh, he's a sharp 'un. As I said before, it's a pity he doesn't belong to us."

While the detective was speaking, Leopold had sat quite still. In the excitement of acting over the scene with Freddy, Barman had scarcely looked at his visitor, but now that it was over he waited to hear some comment upon the story he had just narrated. As Leopold made no reply, the detective raised his eyes and noticed that Leopold was on the point of fainting.

" Hullo, what's this, Sir,—ain't you well?"

Leopold made no reply, but pointed to the bottle of spirits. Quickly comprehending his meaning, Barman poured out a glass of whisky and gave it to his visitor. Leopold drank it off, and then said in a faint voice, which trembled a little in spite of his habitual *sang froid,*—

" I do not feel very well, Mr. Barman,— the fatigue of travelling has been too much for me ; I shall go home. But before I leave you, I want to ask you how long you will take in finishing the case ?"

" Well, Sir," replied the detective, strok-
ing his chin with his palm, " it oughtn't to
be more than a week. You see I shall just
have to rub up my old evidence. Find out
again Mr. Cumberland Kenny at the Paupers' Property Office, and take a run down
to Manchester to learn something of Raymond's antecedents when your father was a
clerk at Tybalt, Smith, and Co.'s. Yes, Sir,
I think I could finish off the job neatly
within a week."

" Then meet me at the Ruthven Arms a
week from hence. And now I must go."

" You still look shaky, Sir. Can't I do
anything for you ?"

" No, thank you ; I am quite recovered.
Show me a light to the door. Thanks ; that
will do. Good-night." And Leopold was
gone. As he walked into the King's Road,
he murmured,—

" Poor girl ! poor, poor girl ! And so
that scoundrel forced her into the marriage
to save her uncle's life. Poor, poor girl !"

As for Barman, he lighted another pipe and ruminated. After the third puff he said, speaking to himself as was his wont when he had no better company,—

"Now, my friend John, I am not best pleased with you! Why not? Because you are letting this young man do a dreadful thing. Why a dreadful thing? You know why well enough. But then, where ignorance is bliss it is folly to be wise, eh, John? Quite so, John, I can't say anything against *that*. And then, again, isn't it a duty to society to run down a murderer? I can't say it isn't, John. Well, then, why are you making such a fuss about it? No nonsense, John; you know why well enough."

And then the detective smoked in silence, looking into the fire and finding shadowy castles in the smoke. After a time he got up to mix a tumbler of spirits and water.

"Well," said he, after taking a gulp of the mixture, "I can't help it,—it would have been agin human nature to have thrown it up. You see it was such a *very* neat affair, and *so* genteel."

And now what was the little servant doing all this while? Why, poor child, she was spelling out a column of an old 'Times,'—a very old 'Times,' dating nearly a month back.

"I do so like these 'ere big letters, 'cause they are easy to make out," said the mite, stumbling over a long word. "Why, I do believe I can make out the whole of this one."

And then she read out to herself aloud the following advertisement, with much show of pride and exultation :—

MISSING.—MR. LEOPOLD LAWSON, who left England three years ago, is requested most earnestly to return at once to S—st—d. If he applies to the Rev. J. D—tt—n he will hear something of the greatest possible importance to his interests.

" Lawks a' mercy," commented the little woman; "'ear something of the greatest possible importance to 'is interests ! 'Ow I *should* like to be Mr. Leopold Lawson !"

CHAPTER V.

SIR RALPH MAKES A CONFESSION.

IT was a cold autumn afternoon. Stelstead was very dreary. The red leaves cumbered the trees, and the wind whistled through the branches with a low angry moan. Not a nice day for walking—scarcely (with the leaden sky and lowering clouds) a pleasant day for riding. In spite of this, Father Dutton marched along the road leading to the new house that has risen from the ashes of the old hall of the Ruthvens,—marched along with a thoughtful brow and a hasty step, looking neither to the right nor the left, but pursuing his course steadily. He passed by the house of Jas Samson, the cobbler, without regarding its inmate as he sat working beside a blazing fire; he passed by the lodge without returning or even noticing the salute of the lodge-keeper; he walked on until he arrived at the hall door. He rang 'the bell and was shown into the library.

"Is Sir Ralph well enough to see me?" he asked.

"Well, Sir, he hasn't passed a very good night," replied the servant who had opened the door for him, "but he gave orders this morning that we were to let him know the moment you arrived. Will you please to wait, Sir?"

"He wants to see me," murmured the priest when he was once more alone. "Why should he wish to see me? He is ill—but he gave up the old religion years and years ago. Surely the rector of the parish would have been a better selection."

And he stood before the window, looking at the dead leaves as they were driven along the terrace by the cold boisterous wind.

"Mr. Dutton, my uncle is very ill; he is excited and nervous. The doctor saw him this morning, and has ordered rest and quiet. For the sake of Heaven do not excite him; remember, he is a sick man."

It was Edith who said this, Edith pale and tearful. She had entered the room noiselessly, and now stood beside the priest, looking up entreatingly into his eyes.

"I have come at your uncle's invitation, Miss Ruthven. My mission is to bring calm to those who suffer, to bind up wounds, not to tear them open."

"I know, I know," she replied quickly; "but he is excited and knows not what he says. He has been very, very good to me! You must not heed his words—indeed you must not."

"Have confidence in me, Miss Ruthven.

I will do your uncle no harm; I will not let harm come near him."

" Not even from his own lips ?"

" Not even from his own lips."

" Oh, thank you! Heaven bless you !" and she seized his hand, and would have raised it impulsively to her lips had he not prevented her.   " I sat beside his bed last night, and as he slept he talked, and I would I had been deaf.   Remember he has been good to me, and I love him.   You hear, I love him!   So be kind, dear Mr. Dutton, and do not listen to his ravings. Mind he is ill and old—very old."

She spoke from her heart, her cheek was flushed with excitement, her bosom rose and fell with her sobs.

" Don't distress yourself, my dear young lady," said the priest, taking her hand and patting it.   " I can make ample allowance for an invalid's fancies."

And then he was summoned by a domestic, and ushered into the sick man's chamber.

Sir Ralph sat in an arm-chair by the side of the fire. He looked up sharply as the priest entered the room, and said in a low voice, which was terrible in its weakness, for it told of decay and death,

" You have come at last; thank God, you have come at last."

And he fell back in his chair, and looked into the fire with lack-lustre eyes. Father Dutton motioned to the servant to withdraw, and then seated himself opposite the baronet.

" You wanted to see me, Sir Ralph?"

" Wanted to see you! I have been dying to see you. Dying. I can't die until I have seen you and have undone the great —the terrible wrong of my youth."

" You have been ill."

" I tell you, man, that I've been dying— that I *am* dying!"

He turned round fiercely, like a wolf at bay, and glared at his visitor.

"Look at me. Don't you see the hand of death stretched over me, ready to fall when atonement, bitter atonement has been made? Ill! Why I have suffered the torments of hell! Ill! Why I would give worlds to lie in my coffin!"

"You must not talk like this," said the priest gravely. "Remember that you are a Christian." Sir Ralph laughed scornfully. "Well, if you will—a man."

"Yes, I am a man, a wretched, miserable, God-forsaken man! And here, with all my sorrows and sins upon my head, I die! Noble destiny! I have lived to breathe, to suffer, and to die!"

"I cannot listen to these words," interrupted Father Dutton. "You were a Catholic once, Sir Ralph, and you know that I cannot, that I may not listen to such words. Have you nothing else to say to me?"

"Nothing else, man! Why have I sent for you; why have I lived to see you; why have I counted the moments that kept you away from me?"

And the old man almost rose from his cushions in his aimless, feverish, peevish excitement. And then the fit left him, and he fell back in his chair, pale and exhausted. The priest waited a moment to allow him to regain his composure, and then said,

"I am here, what do you want with me?"

"I feel that I am dying,—yes, dying, without seeing my poor wronged boy. Has nothing been heard of him; have you found no trace?"

"No, Sir Ralph, none. The advertisement appeared nearly a month ago, and has provoked no answer. I fear that he is indeed lost to us."

"Well, I must not complain. My sin has been heavy, and my punishment cannot be light. Yes, I know the cant—but it is hard, very hard."

The priest made a movement, and half rose from his chair.

"You will not go !" cried Sir Ralph irritably. "You surely will not have the heart to go without waiting to hear the message for my son ?"

"I am here to obey your commands. Speak on, Sir Ralph ; but remember that your words reach the ears of a priest of the Church you have abandoned, of a Church that condemns blasphemers to eternal perdition !"

The baronet leant back heavily in his chair, and seemed to be collecting his thoughts. After a pause of a few minutes he spoke—slowly and with difficulty.

"I feel I am dying, Father Dutton, and what I would have said to my son I must say to you. But you will find him out— you will tell him my words ?"

The priest bowed his head in assent.

"He will learn that I have undone the

wrong I did him at his birth—the wrong of
disowning him—in my will. There he will
find himself acknowledged as my son and
heir : there he will learn his mother's name ;
the church where we were married. I have
written it all. See, here it is. Take this
pen and witness it." The priest obeyed.
"But, oh, I cannot commit to paper the
reason of my sin. You, Father Dutton,
must see him and make him forgive me.
Implore him too—from the bottom of your
heart—with all your soul—on your knees !"

The baronet paused for a moment, passed his hand across his brow, and continued.

" Yes, pray him to forgive me, for I have
wronged him deeply ; and yet I loved him,
loved him dearly."

He paused again, and wiped his lips.

"I was afraid of what I had done. His
mother was so below me in birth. I was
wicked, I was mad ; and my sudden rise to
fortune and title dazzled me. I told her,

God forgive me, that our marriage was a mockery, and broke her heart,—yes, broke her heart!"

The tears gathered in the old man's eyes, and he buried his face in his hands. After a silence of a moment's duration he continued:

"She left me, and I saw her only once again,—in the agonies of death at the workhouse! Yes, poor child, she tried hard to see our son before yielding up her spirit, but it was not to be. She arrived here in Stelstead, but died before he could come to her. She lies buried in the churchyard beside the body of my poor little boy—my second son —Lady Ruthven's child."

He stopped again, and then once more broke the silence that reigned in the chamber.

"When she had left me at Cambridge— brute that I was—I felt a weight lifted from my heart. She was, as I have told you, of very poor parentage, the daughter of a college gyp. Her father was dead; her mother, it was said, had been transported. I was free, quite free, and I enjoyed my liberty, and breathed a new life!"

Again he paused.

"I married a second time; you knew my wife,—Lady Ruthven. Now that I was rich and titled, I could provide for my son and the girl. In the banking house of my bride's father was a young clerk, much addicted to betting. This man robbed the till, was convicted and ruined. When his sentence had expired I found him out, and to him confided the care of my son."

"To him!"

"Yes, to him. I made him live near me, and could have ruined him at any time by revealing his antecedents. I brought up my son as his child."

He paused once more, and after tasting some cooling drink that stood beside him continued:

"For a long time I thought of acknowledging my first born, but when poor little Herbert came to cheer me I changed my mind. It seemed so cruel to deprive the child of its birthright. I was soon punished. Herbert lies buried in yonder churchyard."

He looked towards the window and sighed.

"After the poor child's death, I did not dare to reveal the truth. But I cared for the son that was left to me; I loved him, and treated him as I would have treated him had he been acknowledged my heir."

And now he turned towards the priest and touched his arm.

"As you value the salvation of your soul," he said, "tell him all this, and implore him to forgive me. Point out to him my temptations, enlarge upon my kindness to him when he lived here—in this village. Tell him that I loved his mother to the last; that on her deathbed she forgave me as he must forgive me. Tell him that my life has been a life of sorrow; that even he would pity me if he only knew a tithe of my sufferings. Implore him to forgive me, and if he can to pray for my poor sinful soul."

Sir Ralph was silent. And now the priest rose to depart. He walked towards the door, and then returned and sat down once more beside the baronet.

"Sir Ralph," he said, "you fear your death; have you no fear of meeting your Creator?"

"What do you mean?"

"I mean, are you prepared for death? Can I not help you?"

"Help me—you help me! Do you not know that I am an apostate, as you are a deserter! We have changed sides, gallant soldiers that we are—there is nothing in common between us. Stay; you have given up the faith of your fathers to turn Catholic, as I have spurned the hope of my ancestors to call myself Protestant. Ah, we have one bond of union truly—the bond that binds one traitor to another."

A flush spread over the features of the soldier-priest as he listened to the taunt.

"You wrong me, Sir Ralph," he said. "I listened to the dictates of my conscience. I gave up home, friends, and fortune. Can you say as much?"

The baronet was silent. He sat looking into the fire moodily. By-and-by he turned towards the priest and said, half defiantly, half despairingly,

"There is no hope for me! No, no hope for me!"

"There is hope for every one of us," replied Father Dutton solemnly.

"You are blind!" cried the baronet; "you are blind, dead blind! But come, your Church seals your lips after you have heard a confession. My Church does not forbid me to make one. (Who should know that better than yourself?) Will you hear mine?"

"Yes," said the priest, after a pause; "yes, if it will relieve your mind, if it will lead you to repentance."

"Relieve my mind!" replied Sir Ralph excitedly. "Relieve my mind! Why, man, I have not known a moment's rest, a moment's peace for years. My terrible secret has been too much for me to bear. It has dragged me down, down, down, lower and lower and lower, until now I lie beside the grave helpless, friendless, and hopeless!"

The perspiration drops gathered on his brow, and his eyes shone with an unearthly brightness. The priest shuddered as he watched him.

"I will hear your confession," he said. "Heaven aid me to call you to repentance."

And then he drew a stole from his pocket, and threw it across his shoulders. The baronet laughed scornfully.

"The old tricks," he cried. "The old frippery! And you pretend that you can

forgive me !   You a sinful man like myself
—you !"

" I pretend to nothing," replied the priest.
" You must make your peace above before
you can make your peace with me.   You
need not dread *my* anger, poor creature !"

" Well, go through your forms, seal your
lips to the world, and listen to my story.
You will have need of, all your philosophy
before you have heard me out."

The priest said nothing.   He sat quite
still and waited for his penitent (?) to continue.   Sir Ralph stared into the fire, and
then whispered in a dull, dreadful voice,

" I have been guilty of murder !"

" How many times ?"

A strange question ; a question bordering
on the comic, and yet a natural one.   Yes,
it is on record that a murderer once entered
the confessional and made the same avowal,
and was asked the same question.   " How
many times ?"   No surprise, no horror, only

a profound belief in the wickedness of mankind, in the power of the devil!

"You have done right to ask me that question," said Sir Ralph, looking at the priest for a moment, and then withdrawing his eyes and seeking solace in the red light of the fire. "I murdered Raymond and I murdered John Lawson. Raymond died by my hands, Lawson by the hangman's rope for the crime I alone had committed."

The priest shuddered, and moved away a little from the self-accused murderer.

"You do well to treat me like a leper," whispered the baronet in the same dreadful voice. "Oh, how I have loathed myself since that time! How I have lived I know not. I was mad when I committed the deed; I am mad now!"

He looked drearily into the fire, and continued.

"I was mad—yes, mad. I was mad with jealousy, and the devil was at my elbow. I

was mad with rage! I was mad with pride.
I found him in her chamber at the dead of
night, and I shot him like a dog!"

He paused and wiped the perspiration
from his brow.

" He had been her lover in the early days
when I knew her as the heiress of the banker.
They told me of his love—they hinted that
he held over her a power she dared not defy.
I cared not. She had charms for me that he
had never touched; the charms of a cheque
book—the charms of silver and gold. On
the day of my marriage I saw him—not
again till the hour of his death."

He was silent for a moment, and then continued. The priest sat by his side horror-
stricken.

" The night of Leopold's return from
Oxford, I found a letter addressed to her.
It was from him—from Raymond—making
an appointment to see her that very evening
at a quarter-past eleven. As I read this

cursed letter the clock struck the hour. I scarcely knew what I was doing; my blood coursed through my veins like wild-fire, my temples throbbed. I was mad—yes, I was mad!"

Again he paused.

"On the hall table lay a pistol; it was one I had brought with me from Lawson's house that morning. The gardener had asked me to get one for the ploughboy who guarded the new-sown seed from the birds. I saw this pistol at Lawson's—the man was out—so I brought it with me, intending to tell him that I had borrowed it when next I saw him. Armed with this pistol I went to my wife's chamber. I listened. I heard voices. *He* was there! I called out; my wife answered that she was alone. Mad with rage and jealousy, I left the door and walked out into the grounds. The window of Lady Ruthven's room opened on to the terrace. I walked towards it, and found him on the threshold. I raised my pistol, fired, and killed him!"

He was silent for a moment, and then continued:—

" When the deed was done the excitement left me, and I trembled like a child. *She* was there to succour me. Her pride nerved her; her reputation was at stake. She made me carry the bleeding body of her lover to the spot where it was subsequently found. She put back the hands of the clock, so that I might prove an *alibi*. He had said that he had left the Ruthven Arms at eleven; she put the clock back to that hour. Then she sent me to call the household. She attracted their attention to the time, and made me accompany them in their search, so that I might never be out of their sight—no, not for a moment. You know how and where he was found. When all was quiet she altered the clock once more. You know the rest—you know who was accused, you know who suffered for my crime!"

He was silent, his face resting in his hands, his body shaken by shuddering sobs. The priest rose.

"Ralph Ruthven," he said solemnly, "as you have told me, my lips are sealed to the world. I can never see you again until full atonement has been made. You cannot recall the dead to life; but you *can* clear their memory. If you would make your peace with Heaven, take off the foul stigma attaching to the name of Lawson. Poor wretch, I pity you from my soul! No," he continued, as Sir Ralph held out his hand,— "no, I cannot take it; it is stained with the marks of murder! Wash it clean with prayer and reparation. Make your peace with Heaven, miserable man; make your peace with Heaven!"

And he left him cowering down before the firelight, and the red glare bathed him in a haze that looked like blood!

CHAPTER VI.

"OH, LET ME DIE!"

THE day after the events recorded in the last chapter two travellers arrived by the coach that passed through Stelstead on its way to the county town of Chelmsford. One got out of the interior; the other descended from the box. They both were muffled up to the eyes, and seemed desirous of avoiding any recognition. From his appearance, it was evident that the traveller who had emerged from the interior was many years the junior of the man who had descended from the box. As the "inside" passenger walked into the Ruthven Arms, a waiter touched his hat and said to him,

"Beg your pardon, Sir; but there's a gentleman upstairs, Sir, in the blue-room, who is, I think, a-waiting for you."

The new-comer nodded slightly, and followed the waiter upstairs into a sitting-room.

"Glad to see you, Sir," said a man, rising from his chair, as he entered the apartment. "You see I've kept my appointment. Here, waiter, you can go."

The man took the hint and disappeared.

"Well," said the traveller, throwing off his coat and wrapper and revealing the features of Leopold Lawson—"well, have you completed your case?"

"Yes, Sir," replied the detective, for it was he, "I've got it now as prettily as I can —why, it's quite a pictur'!"

And the two men sat down, and began to talk earnestly and seriously.

In the meanwhile, the "outside" passenger was discussing a hasty meal in the coffee-room. When it was finished he rose up, and asked with a swagger the way to Ruthven Hall.

He was duly directed, and then, with a glance round the room to see what effect his speech had made upon his audience, he took up his walking-stick and swaggered out. Strange to say, in spite of his ignorance of the road, he made very sensible progress; in fact, within a quarter of an hour of his leaving the Ruthven Arms he stood before the hall-door.

" Is Sir Ralph at 'ome ?" he asked, when his summons had been attended to.

" Yes," said the flunkey, eyeing him superciliously—" yes, he's at home, but he ain't well enough to see any one."

" Ah, but 'e will see me," put in the traveller. " You just take up that there bit of cardboard, and see the effect upon 'im."

The flunkey stared and, leaving the traveller in the hall, departed. After a few
minutes he returned, and beckoned him to
follow him. The traveller obeyed, and was
shown into Sir Ralph's chamber.

The baronet did not rise from his chair on
his entrance, but merely motioned the servant to leave them.

When he was gone, he looked at his
visitor and said, "Ah, Dixon, is it you?
You can sit down. What do you want with
me?"

"Ah, Sir Ralph," replied Dixon, *alias*
Cumberland Kenny, *alias* the Controller-in-
Chief of the Paupers' Property Office, "I
ain't all bad—on my word I ain't! When
I came to see you before, it wasn't pleasant
for neither of us. I 'ad to speak pretty sharp,
you know, but then I was just driven to it."

"Well never mind the past. What do
you want with me now?"

"But I do mind the past, Sir Ralph. You

be'aved to me quite 'andsome,—you gev me a sitivation under Government. Which sitivation filled my 'eart with gratitood, Sir Ralph. Which, Sir Ralph, we serv—I means we Government officials 'ave 'earts, Sir Ralph, indeed we 'ave!"

"Well, I am glad you like the place."

"Like the place! Why, it's a beautiful place. No boot-cleaning, no taking up of coals to the drawing-room, no nothing. It's true they don't give yer yer beer and washing; but law, yer mustn't expect everythink, and even them may come some day."

"Well, Dixon, to business. I am very ill, and see no one, but you were such an old—"

"Friend, Sir Ralph—call me friend."

"Such an old servant that I consented to receive your visit. What do you want with me?"

"Well, Sir Ralph," said the other with some hesitation, "I fear I've been a little what I may call injoodicious."

" Injudicious ! How ? "

" Well, Sir Ralph, when one gets a sitivation under Government one MUST launch out. A controller-in-chief can't possibly live upon tripe,—'e can't indeed, Sir Ralph."

" Well ? "

" I got into the 'ands of the Jews, Sir, and they treated me badly—they did, indeed, Sir. Why, if I'd been a junior clerk in my own hoffice, I couldn't 'ave been treated wusser."

" What is all this to lead up to ? Speak up, man, what have you done ? "

" As I said afore, Sir Ralph, I've been injoodicious, werry injoodicious ! To make a long story short, I've been obliged to give up that there letter to Lady Ruthven,—you know the one I means. I was forced to do it, Sir. I'd rather anything 'ad 'appened sooner than that; but I was forced to do it ! "

The baronet sat quite still, but his pallor was terrible to witness. He looked more like a corpse than a breathing man.

"I 'ope you won't take it to 'eart, Sir Ralph," continued the controller uneasily. "I 'ope not, Sir, when I promise you it wasn't my fault."

And now Sir Ralph spoke, but in a very low tone.

"You mean to tell me that you have given up the letter to Lady Ruthven signed by George Raymond ? "

"Yes, Sir Ralph, I'm afeared I have."

"Good God ! "

He was silent for a moment, and then rage took the place of despair.

"And it is for this I have bribed and petted you! It is for this that I have forgotten my own honour, and have given you, miserable churl that you are, a post destined for gentlemen ! "

"No, Sir Ralph, you are a-going a deal too . far. Call me any names you please, accuse me as much as ever you like, but don't go for to say that a sitivation in the

Paupers' Property Office is a fit thing for a gentleman—'cause atween ourselves, it ain't."

The baronet relapsed into silence, and gazed moodily out of the window. After a while, without turning his head, he asked in a fierce tone,

"Whom did you give the letter to?"

"Well, Sir Ralph, that's the worst part of it; I'm almost afeared I guv that there letter to a detective."

"A detective!"

The words seemed to crush him down. He hid his face in his hands. Ah! it was a pitiable sight; even the ex-flunkey was moved.

"It ain't so bad as you think, Sir Ralph," he said. "It was a many years ago when I guv it up, and I shouldn't 'ave mentioned it now only that there man came to me a day or so ago and began to question me about this and that. 'E didn't get much out of

me this time though. Still I thought as
'ow I ought to let you know, Sir Ralph.
That's why I took the liberty of coming,
Sir."

The baronet did not look at him, but
merely motioned to him to go.

Oh certainly, Sir Ralph, if you desire it,"
said the controller, bridling up. " I'm sure
I don't want to intrude, Sir Ralph. Not at
all. Good morning, Sir."

And he was gone. The old man trembled
in every limb, and seemed stricken with a
mortal terror.

" Dragged to the scaffold," he cried, " in
my old age. Dragged to the scaffold now
that I am old !"

He was so overwhelmed with despair and
grief that he did not notice another visitor
to his room, who stood regarding him with
an expression denoting sorrow and yet firm-
ness. It was Leopold Lawson—Leopold the
avenger !

" Sir Ralph, I must speak with you."

The baronet started and looked up with age-bedimmed eyes.

" Who are you?" he asked peevishly. " Who gave you leave to come here—into my chamber—when I am ill?"

" Who gave me leave?" the other echoed in a cold cruel voice. " Who gave me leave to seek you here—to appear before you as an avenger and a judge? who gave me leave to do all this and more? *You* ask me! I will tell you—the dead—the murdered dead!"

The baronet made an effort to move from his chair and tried to reach the bell-rope.

" No, you are wrong," continued his visitor. " I am not mad. My words shall be few, but to the point. The time has come to tell you some plain truths, Sir Ralph— to drag you from your position down to the dregs of the people—among the felons— among the murderers!"

The old man shrank back in mortal terror. The other stood over him like the figure of Nemesis—cold, determined, and heartless. He stood there denouncing him with all the fire of an enthusiast, with all the force of a monomaniac.

" It should have been done before," he cried, "and I have been punished—deeply punished—for the delay. Sir Ralph, you are a murderer—a double murderer. You murdered George Raymond with your own hand; you murdered John Lawson with your silence.'"

Again the baronet attempted to rise, and fell back once more from pure exhaustion.

" Ah, I see," said his visitor in the same voice; " you judge my words to be the ravings of a maniac, but I tell you you are wrong. Yes, and you shall learn that you are wrong. It would be better for both of us that I were indeed mad—much better."

He paused for a moment, as if a feeling of

deep regret were crossing o'er his mind, and
then resumed once more the thread of his address with a cold determination that told of
a supreme act of will.

"You think I have no warranty for my
words. Well, we will see. See if I cannot
lead you step by step to the scaffold! Years
and years ago, Sir Ralph, Raymond, the
murdered man, loved your wife. She was
not your wife then, but still you quarrelled
with her for this very love. You defy me
to prove it? The partner of your father-in-
law, Tybalt, will prove it—has proved it.
Step the first!"

He stopped and looked at the old man.
For a moment he struggled with some strong
emotion, and then mastering it, continued
his narrative, but without looking again at
the object of his denunciation.

"You married Lady Ruthven, and for
years no more was heard of Raymond. But
one day this old lover of your wife, this

Raymond, returned to her. He wrote a letter to her—a shameful letter if you will—that letter fell into your hands, and that letter was the cause of his death. You defy me to prove it? I have the letter, I have witnesses who know that it reached your hands. Step the second!"

Again he paused, but only for a moment.

"At the trial of your second victim, John Lawson, you counted upon an *alibi* to save *your* neck and to endanger *his*. You tried to prove that the murder was committed while you were actually in the house, attended by your servants, searching for the murdered man,—at the time when the murdered man was alive—at his inn. Your false proof goes for nothing. You defy me to gainsay it? Lady Ruthven was seen to put the clock on a couple of hours immediately after the murder. Seen by a witness who is prepared to prove it. Step the third!"

Again he paused. Sir Ralph sat quite still, his face full of horror, his eyes starting from his head, his hands clenched in mortal agony.

Leopold continued in the same cold, determined tone.

"But this is not enough—you would hear more — then listen. Near the murdered man was found a pistol, attached to this pistol a label inscribed with the name of John Lawson. This pistol was seen in your possession on the day of the murder by one of the ploughboys. He was too young to know the value of his evidence *then*. You defy me to prove this? It has been proved before the magistrates. Sir Ralph Ruthven, the warrant for your apprehension on the charge of wilful murder is even now in the hands of the officers. Step the last!"

He paused, and then, approaching the baronet more closely, spoke yet a few words more.

"I have not done. You must learn who it is that has thus hunted you down—who has brought you to justice—who has led you to the foot of the scaffold. Remember you had no pity upon *him*; you let him hang like a dog when by a word you could have saved him. And he in return has left it to me to deal out a fearful retribution— to hang you, you hear, even as you let him hang! It was a fearful legacy, but I have accepted it, and my father's murder will be at length avenged!"

"Your father's murder!" Oh! what an unearthly cry!

"Yes, my father's murder! My name is Leopold Lawson. So changed by sorrow that you did not recognize me! Leopold Lawson, do you hear! Now you know what mercy you may expect from me!"

As Leopold stood over him, the baronet caught the young man's hand, and burst into a passionate fit of weeping. So bitter, so full of awful sorrow, that no pen can e'er describe it.

"Unhand me!" cried Leopold. "How dare you touch me! Do you not hear who I am?" And he cast the old man roughly from him.

There was a pause, and then came the fearful words.

"Leopold, my son, my only son! Is it thy hand—thy hand that will kill thine own father! Oh, let me die! oh, let me die! oh, let me die!"

CHAPTER VII.

A DESPERATE GAME.

JOHN BARMAN sat in the coffee-room at the Ruthven Arms. He tapped impatiently on the table, and grumbled not a little.

"I have done wrong," said he; "I ought to have gone myself. I can't trust him—if he does but find out. Well, anyhow, I've got the warrant pretty safe, that's one comfort."

But he continued to tap upon the table, and seemed anything but satisfied. As he pursued his occupation, a "loudly" dressed man entered the room, and rushed to the bell-handle and pulled at it vigorously. When the "loudly" dressed man turned round, he found Mr. Barman in the depths of a newspaper. The "loudly" dressed one "hem'd" and "hawed," and murmured something about the inattention of waiters.

"Beg your pardon, gentlemen, I'm sure," said the landlord, bustling in, "rather busy day—market going on. Can I get you anything, gentlemen?"

"*I* rang," said the "loudly" dressed "gentleman," pompously. "What 'ave you in the kitchen?"

"Almost everything, Sir," replied the landlord, with a rustic bow. "That's to say, I *know* there's some eggs, and I *think* there's some bacon."

"Bring me, then, some of your best eggs and some of your finest bacon, a chop if you've got one, a quart of ale, and some cheese," said the "loudly" dressed traveller, with much dignity. "I don't mind what I pay (up to eighteenpence) so long as it's good.   You understand."

The host smiled and went out to give the order.

"P'raps, Sir," continued he of the gorgeous apparel, "when you've *quite* done with that there paper, you will let me 'ave a look at it."

"You can have it now, Mr. Cumberland Kenny, if you want it," said Barman.

"Law, bless me, Mr. Barman!" cried the controller, "'oo ever would a' thought of seeing *you* 'ere!"

"Quite an unexpected· pleasure, Mr. Kenny, ain't it? You see your little game was quite spoilt.   Yes, Sir, we've got down here as soon as you."

"Wot little game, Mr. Barman?"

"Oh, you know very well, Mr. Kenny. You don't want to see your golden goose killed, eh?   You prefer the eggs to the carcase.   Oh, we *quite* understand you, Mr. Kenny!"

"I don't know nothing about it, Mr. Barman; but there, you always would have your joke. But see," he added, as the host brought in some eatables, "here's some eggs and bacon. Won't you join me in a friendly pick?"

"Well, Mr. Kenny, I generally *do* draw the line at the hangman; but an occasion is —in point of fact—an occasion."

The two worthies sat down to their lunch. Barman nodded to the host.

"Well, landlord, how's the world been treating you?"

"Very nicely indeed, Sir.   Lost my wife."

"That's sad."

"Well, Sir, as to that, it's a matter of taste. Poor woman, some one told me the other day that she was dead, so I mustn't abuse her."

"Why, didn't she die here?"

"No, Sir. They say she ran away with

a commercial traveller, but I don't think she did. In fact, I've a good proof to the contrary."

" Have you ?"

" Yes, Sir. She told me she would run away with him. Now, as I never knew her once to keep her word, I say the whole story must be false."

" Did you take any notice about the matter afterwards ?"

" I should think I did, Sir ! Why, I didn't speak to that commercial traveller for more than a month ! "

" You will be marrying again soon, I suppose ?"

" Not I, Sir. No, that's the pull we widowers have over the bachelors. One seldom catches the scarlet fever or marriage more than once, thank goodness ! "

And with this sage remark the landlord left the room.

The meal progressed. Barman was gruff

and uncommunicative,—Kenny civil, but nervous. When it was over, the latter got up, and bidding the detective adieu, paid his score and walked off to meet the afternoon coach to Chelmsford.

After he had gone, Barman stirred the fire and lighted a short pipe. He divided his time between smoking, drinking, and grumbling. Every now and then he rose from his chair and approached the window, and looked out into the road. After having done this for the third time, he murmured as he resumed his seat:

"At last, but the gaff is blown. I can see it in his face. John Barman, you must be firm; mind, the warrant is issued."

With this he puffed away at his pipe in silence. In a moment more Leopold Lawson entered the room and sat down beside the fire. Leopold's face was pale, very pale, his lips were colourless, and his hand trembled.

"Barman," he said; "Barman."

"Ah, there you are, Sir. Made it all right with the old gentleman? Well, now you've had your whim, we must come to serious business. I must take him to-night."

"Barman, the happiness of my life depends upon your answer, I want to ask you something."

"I'm sure I would be very happy to oblige you, Sir, in anything that didn't interfere with my dooty."

"Barman, if I offered you a thousand pounds; if I begged and implored of you to accept them, would you save yonder old man's life? I ask but for twelve hours' grace, then do what you will."

"If you guv me £100,000 it would be no good now, Sir. The warrant is in my hands, and it is as much as my reputation's worth to let him escape. It can't be done, Sir."

"But you don't know all, man," cried Leopold in an agony. "This old man is my father,—do you hear, my own father!"

"Well, Sir, excuse me," said the detective coolly, "but I suspected as much. The fact was, I travelled one day with a parson who attended Lawson at his execution, he said something about it."

"And you have let me hunt down my own father!"

"Well, Sir," replied the detective with something like a blush, "you see you was werry positive. Says I to you, 'Don't you do it;' says you, 'I will! It ain't no business of yours,' nor more it were. So you see that's how it came about, Sir."

"Oh, man, man, have you no heart?"

"Well, Sir, I'm werry sorry I'm sure if you're disappinted. But, law bless you! we will do it as genteelly as possible. Get the old gentleman quietly before the magistrates, keep the doors closed, and no one

need know anything about it until the ses-
sions. There, I can't say fairer than that."

"Will nothing move you?"

"Nothing, Sir; that's flat. Let's say no
more about it; you're only distressing yourself, and you ain't doing no manner of
good."

Leopold was silent for a moment, and
then he cried out,

"I believe you are right. How has he
treated me, this father of mine! Disowned
me, let me starve for what he cared! You
are right, Barman; he shall not escape, no,
no, he shall not escape!"

The detective looked up sharply at the
young man and thought to himself, "Is this
gammon, I wonder?" He said nothing
however, but listened to hear what would
next fall from Leopold's lips.

"Yes!" cried the junior after a short
pause. "Why should I show pity where
none has been shown to me? You say right,

Barman; he shall be arrested this very evening. Come, let us drink a bottle of wine and then go up to the Hall together."

He got up and rang the bell. His face was flushed, and he seemed half mad with excitement. When his summons was answered by the landlord, he ordered some sherry, some ink, some note paper, and a pen to be brought to him.

"I want to write a line to an old friend," he explained with a laugh; "after the wine it may not be so easy to send it. Eh?"

"Well, Sir," replied the landlord, "if you've a weak head at all, I'd advise you to take some of our brandy. I don't pretend to be a judge of wine, but I have been told that our cogniac is much weaker than our sherry."

This was said with much pride. After a while the landlord arrived with the things ordered. Leopold caught up a pen and dashed off a line on a piece of paper.

" I won't be a moment, Barman," he said.
"And now, landlord, see that this note is
taken to that address immediately."

The host of the Ruthven Arms bowed and
departed on his errand.

" There," said Leopold, filling two glasses,
"let's make ourselves comfortable. There's
nothing like wine for steadying the nerves.
I learnt that in Australia."

Again the detective looked at him, but
with less suspicion this time. " He wants
to get drunk, so that he may carry it out
with spirit. Well, it is rather a twister,
hanging your own father—not that I ever
had one—if I had, I 'spose he would have
been hanged." With this strange reflection,
he sat looking into the fire.

The conduct of the two men showed a
marked difference. The younger talked in-
cessantly, while the elder preserved a gloomy
silence. The first bottle discussed, Leopold
ordered a second. Barman seemed satisfied

to drink a glass against glass with his enter-
tainer, and by degrees the wine began to
tell upon him. His face relaxed, his tongue
loosened, and soon, encouraged by Lawson,
he began to tell stories of his career,—how
he got up this divorce case, how he discovered that murder. He abused the times,
and deplored the decrease of crime in piteous
accents.

"The profession ain't what it was, Sir, I
give you my word of honour," he said
solemnly. "You would scarcely believe it,
but we ain't had a case of poisoning these
three years. Since Sir Ralph's little affair
(which, mind you, is a very clever bit of
business) we haven't had anything worthy
of an ordinary London policeman, much
more of a first-class detective."

At this moment the landlord opened the
door, and told Leopold that there was a
gentleman who wanted to see him.

"I shan't be a second, Barman," said

Lawson, rising. "Just finish the bottle while I'm away. We'll have another when I come back."

Then, with rather an unsteady step he left the room. "Poor young fellow!" murmured Barman when he was gone, "buying Dutch courage, eh? Well, it certainly is a twister," and he helped himself to another glass of sherry.

Leopold found Jas Samson waiting . for him. He shook hands warmly with the old cobbler, and looked inquiringly at him.

"Yes," said the old man, "I got your letter. You'll find the trap at the door—I've got the best horse I could. God bless you, my dear boy."

Leopold called for a tumbler of cold water, drained it, and as he shook hands with Samson once more, whispered,

"Keep him as long as you can, Jas. Every moment is of importance."

And then he sprang into the dog-cart that

he found waiting for him at the door, and drove off sharply as the clock of the village church was striking four.

The fresh country air soon revived him. By the time he reached the park gates the effects of the wine he had drunk had disappeared. Galloping the horse up the avenue, he gained admittance to the Hall at once.

" Is he ready ?" he asked of Edith, who, pale and resolute, stood at the door, awaiting his arrival.

" Yes," she answered ; and then a muffled figure was helped into the trap, and Leopold took his seat once more.

" Good-bye, dear ; good-bye, Leopold !"

" Good-bye, Edith !"

And the whip cracked sharply, and the dog-cart rolled away. Down the avenue, past the park gates, out of sight.

*   *   *   *   *   *

In the meanwhile Jas Samson had entered the coffee-room at the Ruthven Arms.

" You don't recollect me, Mr. Barman ?"

" Yes, I do," replied the detective. " You're the cobbler; you were a close card, eh ? Law, I never forget a face !"

The landlord appeared carrying a third bottle of sherry.

" Eh ?" said Barman, rather confusedly. " I say, I think I've had enough."

" Not you !" cried Samson, heartily. " Here, fill up your glass,—see, I fill mine, —and that's for Mr. Lawson ; he'll be here directly."

And the anecdotes recommenced. Talking is dry work, so it was not surprising that a fourth bottle appeared after the third was finished, and a fifth after the fourth, this time accompanied by a pair of lighted candles.

" Wheresh Mishter Lawshon ?" at last asked the detective.

" Well, to tell you the truth, he's gone to bed," replied the cobbler, who had been much more sparing of the bottle than his companion. "I did not like to say so, for fear of making you uncomfortable about drinking your fair share. The fact is, he's got a weak head—always had."

"But he'sh a cool hand," said the detective, with a drunken laugh. "Hangsh his own fathersh! Hangsh his own fathersh!"

"Quite so!" assented the cobbler.

"Thatsh remind me," cried Barman, with sudden gravity. "Serve warrant—musht do it at once. Take Shir Ralph into cushtody! I shay in cushtody!"

"To be sure. I'll go with you, if you like."

"You're good fellowsh; I like you." He rose unsteadily. "How the room goesh round. John Barman—I shay—John Barman, you're drunk, beastly 'toxicated. I'm 'shamed of you, John Barman!"

The cobbler offered the detective his arm, which was immediately accepted.

" I tell you what it is, Mishter Shamson,"
continued Barman, "the Raymond murder,
—pretty piece of bushness—genteel piece of
bushness ! I'm proud of it. Itsh been
managed capitally—I shay capitally !"

" Quite so," assented the cobbler, and the
two friends went out together. They took
the road to Ruthven Hall. The clock of the
village church struck nine as they entered
the park gate.

CHAPTER VIII.

FREDDY IS JEALOUS.

MORNING was breaking in London. Heavy, lumbering market waggons were arriving in Covent Garden, early steamboats to Boulogne and Rotterdam and Antwerp were departing from London Bridge. The beggars were waking, and crawling from the arches and the doorsteps. The lamplighters were turning off the gas, now superfluous in the glare of the rising sun. All was preparation for the coming day.

There were not many lodgers at the Terminus Hotel on this particular morning, and of the few who were staying at that world-famed hostelrie, there were at least two who were already stirring, an old man and a young man. As the clock struck six, the young man descended the stairs of the hotel, and giving orders to a waiter to have breakfast ready in a quarter of an hour, walked on to the platform of the station. He strolled up to a board containing the time-tables of most of the railways, and finding Euston Square, passed his finger down the list until he came to Liverpool.

"Five hours," he murmured, "and the boat starts at four this afternoon. He must go on board at once."

As he looked at the placard he heard the noise of steam, the voices of excited porters, and the clattering of cabs. Turning round, he found that the tidal train had arrived from Folkestone. As it still wanted five minutes to complete the quarter of an hour required for the preparation of breakfast, he walked up and down the platform watching the passengers.

A motley crowd. Old ladies, and their daughters, and maids—the ladies minus rouge, the daughters without chignons, the maids requiring soap and water. Then there were young Englishmen who seemed surprised at seeing the sun at such an early hour, and who abandoned their travelling caps on arriving at the platform to assume the regulation Lincoln and Bennett. Then there were fat Frenchmen, very dirty and much excited, who were seized upon by unprincipled cabmen, and driven off in triumph to the realms of Leicester Square. Then there were disagreeable "fathers of families" who, one felt sure, would write letters to the 'Times' on the slightest provocation, and servants looking after their masters' luggage, and nurses carrying infant lords and embryo marquises. And there was a good deal of confusion and chattering, and bad French and worse English, and then the cabs came

into requisition and the excitement subsided.
At last, of all the arrivals, only one remained
—a young Englishman.

He was not particularly prepossessing; in
fact, there was something peculiarly "ruffish"
in his appearance. He was "loudly" dressed,
and carried a small carpet-bag. His face
was pale, and told eloquently of drink and
dissipation. His step was bold, his gaze
defiant; but then the boldness was the hero-
ism of the swindler,—the defiance, the fear-
lessness of the outcast of society.

As our breakfast-orderer turned to walk
back to the hotel, he met this amiable-look-
ing youth face to face.

" Holston !"

" Harwood !"

They regarded one another with great
surprise, and then Freddy said calmly,

" I want a word with you, as you may
imagine. Is there any private room where
we can speak without being disturbed ?"

"I can give you just three minutes," said Leopold, looking at his watch.

They walked into the First-class Waiting room.   Leopold sat down, Freddy stood before him.

"Harwood, or Lawson, or whatever your confounded name is," Holston began, in a cold bitter voice, which told of the suppressed passion of the speaker, "I hated you the first time I ever met you.   I hated you and despised you when I found you in love with Florence; hated you and loathed you when I helped to hang your father!"

"Holston!" cried Leopold, springing to his feet.

"Oh yes, strike me!" continued Freddy, in the same calm voice.   "Strike me, coward and bully that you are.   Strike me in all your strength and youth.   Strike me as I stand before you weak from drink and illness, —it will be a safe victory, and one to boast of afterwards."

"What do you mean?" said Leopold, letting his arm fall by his side. "Speak on, but I warn you do not provoke me too much."

"What do I mean? Why this, I robbed you of Florence."

"Don't mention her name."

"But I will mention her name. I robbed you of Florence. My wife Florence. Do you hear, my wife? But I robbed you of her fairly."

"Yes, very fairly. You played the uncle against the niece. But let that pass—she is your wife."

"Leopold Lawson, you insulted me once, and I showed myself a coward. Why? Because then I had something to live for— to hope for. If it was only to cut you out with Florence, that was something. But now that brandy is my only god, and an empty pocket my constant companion, I've learnt to be brave. By Heaven, I'll fight you!"

"Are you drunk, Holston?" said Leopold, surprised beyond measure at this strange address. "What does all this mean?"

"Why this. Coward, thief that you are, you have robbed me of my wife!"

Leopold stared at him in open-mouthed astonishment.

"Don't seek to deny it. The very evening that I dined with you at Wiesbaden, Florence left me. She—"

"Florence has left you!" cried Leopold. "Do you mean to say that she is wandering over the face of the earth defenceless and friendless?"

"No, I mean to say nothing of the sort. I know very well that she is with you— that—"

"Stop!" cried Lawson. "I tell you you lie! Poor girl—poor girl!"

The sorrow of Leopold was so genuine that Freddy could not believe any longer in the base, degrading suspicion that he had adopted before meeting him. He changed his tone, and recounted the story of Florence's flight. Leopold said not a word, but listened intently. When Freddy had finished, Lawson rose from his chair and walked towards the door. Freddy followed him.

" Leave your address at Royal Chambers. I shall be in town again in the course of a a few days."

" Very well." And then Freddy continued in a low tone, that was intended to be pathetic, " I am sorry for this disagreeable meeting after so pleasant a *téte-à-téte* at Wiesbaden—very sorry. By the bye, could you lend me a tenner until we meet again ?"

Leopold threw him a bank-note as he would have thrown a bone to a cur, and then he left the room.

Freddy lounged out and walked into the refreshment room of the station and ordered some breakfast.

As he discussed the meal he thought over his conversation with Leopold.

"His surprise seemed genuine enough," he said; "and, after all, her letter doesn't look like running away with him."

He drew out of his pocket the letter that Florence had left for him at Wiesbaden on the day of his dinner with Leopold.

"'I shall never see you again,'" he read. "'When you receive this I may be dead—yes, death is preferable to a life of misery with you.' What stuff women write!"

By this time he had finished his breakfast, so after paying for it with a part of the ten pound note he rose from the table and walked on to the platform.

"He must be staying here," he murmured; "I may as well ask after him."

Upon this he lounged into the office of the hotel and describing Leopold, asked if he was accompanied by any one on his departure.

"Oh, yes!" said a very haughty young female. "They went away five minutes ago—a lady and gentleman."

Freddy started back. He had been deceived after all. He hurried out and met the hall porter, slipping a shilling into the man's hand, he said,

"Two passengers left five minutes ago?"

"Yes, Sir, a young gentleman and a—"

"Yes, yes. Where did they go?"

"To Euston Square, Sir. The young gentleman told the cabman to look sharp as they wanted to catch the 8.15 train to Liverpool."

Freddy threw himself into a Hansom and told the driver to drive for his life to "Euston Square."

"You will never catch that train, Sir," said the hall porter.

"I will try."

And the cab rattled away.

*   *   *   *   *   *

"Love," said the companion of the haughty young female who had given Freddy his information, " you made a mistake just now. That rackety-looking chap wanted No. 24 and 25, the young man with the white hair and his pa, and you told him 79—the bridal party, love."

" Did I, dear ?" replied the haughty young female coolly. " Well, it's his own fault. The public oughtn't to bother !"

CHAPTER IX.

JUSTICE, THE PURSUER!

IN spite of all the efforts of the cabman, Freddy arrived too late for the train to Liverpool. He cursed his luck in no measured language, and then asked the porter when the next train would leave.

" The next train to Liverpool, 11.5," and the man hurried away.

" Three hours to wait," murmured Freddy. " Well, what can't be cured must be endured."

And with this very philosophical reflection he left the station.

"What shall I do?" he said to himself and looked round. A public-house caught his eye. "The very thing! A glass of brandy will do me no harm; it's precious cold."

With this, he entered the tavern and, walking into the parlour, ordered some spirits and water.

"Ah, this is the stuff to put life and soul into a fellow!" he exclaimed, when the brandy was brought to him. "Bring me another glass, my dear."

The barmaid tossed her head at the familiar address, and sailed out of the room (which was separated from the bar by a glazed partition) with much show of anger and disdain.

"His dear indeed!" she said, as she regained her place behind the beer engines,— "his dear indeed! I never saw such imperence!"

And she tossed her head and was very

wroth, — being virtuous as all barmaids should be, and ugly as all barmaids are.

"I beg your pardon," said a soft voice, "but please would you—"

"Buy some matches? No, we won't!"

It was a poor young woman, in a very shabby dress, who had addressed the virtuous barmaid. The poor young woman had golden hair and blue eyes, and thin hands and pale cheeks,—a very poor young woman indeed.

"I am not a beggar," said the intruder, with a faint blush. "I am a governess."

"Oh, then, *in course* you are not a beggar,—not yet a pauper,—*in course* not!" The virtuous barmaid could be very severe when she was in a bad temper.

The poor woman turned round and made towards the door, when the barmaid (who, in spite of her sharp tongue, had a good heart), cried after her,

"Lord bless you, my dear, don't cut up

rough! Don't you see I'm upset? What can I do for you?"

"I merely wanted to ask the way to Laurel Cottage, Malvern Road," replied the poor woman. "I am a stranger here and none of the shops are open, and—"

"When are you going to bring my brandy-and-water?" said Freddy, appearing at the door leading to the bar. "You know, my dear, I can't wait all day."

"You must wait, Sir. I've other people to attend to before you," snapped out the barmaid; and then she turned round to give the required directions to the poor woman— in vain.

The governess had started when she heard Freddy's voice, and when he appeared at the bar she had turned round sharply, and had left the tavern.

"Nice manners, I do think," commented the angry barmaid, when she found that the woman had gone. "It's my belief she only came into the place to steal a pewter pot!"

And she tossed her head, and carried in to Freddy the spirits he had ordered.

"Betsy, my love," said the amiable youth, "you may have a glass too if you like."

"My name isn't Betsy, Sir," exclaimed the barmaid indignantly, "and I'll thank you to keep your distance. As for the brandy, I never drink at *this* place!"

And she bounced off. Holston stayed for a couple of hours smoking and drinking, and then rose to leave. He paid his score, walked to Euston Square, and threw himself into a first-class carriage bound for Liverpool.

In due course the train arrived at its destination, and Freddy sobered by a couple of hours' sleep, got out. His first care was to question the station officials. Had they seen, he asked, a young man with whitish hair travelling with a young lady? No they hadn't, not one of them. Here; there was a gentleman with white hair who had arrived by the morning train, but *he* was not accompanied by a young lady; of that they were all of them *quite* sure.

After this futile attempt, Freddy left the station and called at several of the principal hotels, with no better success. The young lady with blue eyes and golden hair was a myth so far as the Liverpudlians were concerned, that was evident.

" I've made an ass of myself," said Freddy, after the eighth failure. "That stupid hall porter must have made a mistake. Well, it doesn't matter, I may as well be here as anywhere."

And he walked about the town, admiring its numerous (?) beauties. As he passed by the docks many a flaring placard met his gaze — one particularly attracted his attention. It ran as follows :—

Will Sail on the — *October*, 18—,

THE FAVOURITE PASSENGER SHIP,

"THE COLUMBIA."

CAPTAIN HAWKINS.

A 1; 2000 tons register.

BOUND FOR NEW YORK.

N.B.—Passengers will be taken on board at 4 p.m.
on the day of sailing by a steamer from the —— Pier.

"Shouldn't care very much about going away on such a day as this," said Freddy, looking up into the sky. "Nasty wind— there will be a tempest to-night, if my eyes don't deceive me."

And he walked on. By-and-by the pangs of thirst began to make themselves felt, and he sought relief in a public-house. "Brandy, and nothing but brandy," seemed to be his motto. In the course of an hour or so he was once more drunk. Sad, but true!

In this degrading state he walked towards the river, and found himself close to — Pier. The 'Columbia,' with her sails loosened, lay in the river ready to start at a moment's notice. As he sleepily watched the preparations for departure, the steamboat neared the pier, and the passengers for the ' Columbia ' began to embark.

He made a few unsteady steps towards the landing-place, when he was seized roughly by the arm by a policeman.

" Hold up, Sir," said the official. " If you don't take care, you'll be in the water. If you'll take my advice, you'll go to bed."

" I am all right, policeman," he replied, with hiccoughy dignity. " I am not drunk, I 'sure you."

" Of course not, Sir," assented the constable with a smile, " any one can see that with half an eye."

And the man moved away. Freddy leant against a post, lazily watching the passengers as they walked on board the steamer. Just as the sailors were loosening the ropes that kept the boat beside the pier, a coach drove up to the landing-place. The coachman opened the door and let down the steps, and then two men descended—one was young, the other old. The driver was paid, and the passengers made for the steamboat. Freddy allowed them to pass him, but when they had walked down the short pier and had embarked, the elder turned round as if he would gaze once more at his native land —perhaps for the last time.

In a moment Holston had recognized Sir Ralph Ruthven!

Half sobered by the sight, he sprang forward, and shouting out "Murder," rushed down the pier.

"Stop him," he screamed at the top of his voice; "he is escaping! He is a murderer, I tell you! Stop him! Do you hear, stop him!"

Those who saw him took him for a maniac, and tried to seize him. Eluding their clutches he arrived at the end of the pier as the steamer was moving slowly away. He took a desperate leap and fell short—into the water.

Before anything could be done to save him he rose to the surface, was caught in the paddle-wheel, drawn up by it, and beaten and crushed against the paddlebox; then the engines were stopped and his body fell once more into the water.

Quick as thought a boat was lowered, and he was dragged out of the river by a dozen eager hands. He was taken on board the steamer—was laid on the deck. A crowd collected round him, and one man knelt down by his side and raised his arm, it fell back like lead; felt his heart, it did not beat.

Yes, Freddy Holston was dead!

*   *   *   *   *   *

It was a fearful night. The 'Columbia' bore up bravely against the tempest, but it was a terrible trial for her. Her timbers creaked and groaned as every wave dashed against her sides with the force of an avalanche; her masts bent before the wind, and her sails were torn to ribbons.

On deck everything was confusion; the sailors rushed hither and thither, obeying the orders of their officers. At last, there was heard a terrible crash, and the poor passengers thought that their last hour had come—that the ship must sink. A terrible night indeed.

Sir Ralph sat in his cabin, musing over the events of the past twenty-four hours. He thought of his son—the dear son he had so longed to recover—the son who had been found at last only to be lost to him for ever. He thought of Edith, of Florence, of all the friends he had ever known, of Stelstead. And as he mused he heard the words, " Lost for ever, lost for ever " ringing in his ears. By degrees he grew drowsy,—nature claimed her own, and he fell asleep.

When he woke it was broad daylight.

To his surprise the 'Columbia' was apparently sailing in calm water. He offered up a prayer of gratitude for his deliverance from a shameful death, and then hurried on deck. To his astonishment he found one of the masts gone. He went up to the officer of the watch and spoke to him.

"A terrible storm last night."

"Yes, very bad weather indeed. We lost our mainmast."

"It's very calm now."

"So it should be—we are in the river."

"What!" said Sir Ruthven trembling with terror. "Are—we—not—"

"Going on? Oh dear, no. We are going back to Liverpool to refit."

CHAPTER X.

A STRANGE DREAM!

THE disabled 'Columbia' was towed to Liverpool. The passengers were none of them displeased to see their native land— their friends—once again. With an exception; Sir Ralph sat moody, numbed with terror—hopeless—almost senseless. As the busy sailors passed him, he regarded them with a meaningless stare. It was a painful sight.

Soon Liverpool was neared, and then a little boat was observed to make for the ship. The little boat seemed to grow larger as it approached the vessel, and at length was safely moored by the side of the 'Columbia.' A man sprang on deck and asked for the captain.

"I am the senior officer of this ship," said the official in question. "Captain Hawkins—that's my name."

"Glad to see you, Captain Hawkins; and to return the compliment, my name's Barman, of the Detective Force."

"Happy to make your acquaintance," Sir, returned Hawkins courteously. "Can I do anything for you?"

"Nothing particular, Captain, except a little case of murder!"

"Murder!" exclaimed the commanding officer of the 'Columbia,' in a tone of disgust. "Ah, the service is going to the devil when murderers actually have the impertinence to take passages! I *did* think we drew the line at fraudulent bankrupts (who have been very numerous since the crisis); but murderers, it's too bad! It really is a great deal too bad!"

"Oh, you need not take the matter to heart!" said Barman, bridling up at the disrespectful tone in which the captain had spoken of his capture. "My man is a baronet,—he belongs to one of the oldest families in Essex."

"Really!" exclaimed the Captain. "Well, certainly, that does make a difference. A titled murderer is certainly better; but still, I have an aversion (unreasonable possibly in this case) to criminals. I suppose you have a warrant with you?"

"Here it is, Sir," promptly returned the detective, producing the document in question.

Hawkins put on his glasses, and calmly read the warrant through.

"Sir Ralph Ruthven!" he murmured. "Fine old family, Sir; fine old family!"

"Yes," assented Barman with professional

pride. "The whole case is very genteel, I might say, very genteel indeed. I suppose I may look for my man?"

"Oh, certainly." And the search commenced.

Barman soon found Sir Ralph. The baronet was sitting, as has been described, beside the bulwarks. The detective approached him and, touching him on the shoulder, told him that he was his prisoner on the charge of murder.

"And it's my duty to tell you to be careful of what you say, Sir, as it may be used against you. And now, Sir, if you've no objection, we'll just slip on this pair of bracelets."

"Spare me that!" cried the baronet, shrinking away from the detective; "oh, spare me that!"

"You don't like 'em, Sir Ralph? Well, it is strange, but all real gentlemen *do* have an objection to them, and yet they are as easy and as comfortable as can be. Why, they'd please a babby !"

" Spare me—spare me !" repeated the baronet, in a dull, dreary voice.

" Well, Sir, I always like to make myself agreeable to parties, especially in genteel cases, and if you will just let me catch hold of your arm in this kind of way, it will do quite as well. And now, Sir, we must look sharp and get into the boat."

Barman and his prisoner quickly descended the side of the vessel, and were soon on their way back to Liverpool. The detective carried on the conversation by himself.

" You mustn't mope, Sir,—indeed you mustn't. The storm certainly was disappointing, but, law bless you, Sir, we should have caught you on the other side as safely as possible. Of that you may be quite sure."

The baronet said nothing; he was staring

into vacancy. His constant thought was, "They will hang me—they will hang me!"

"It may be all for the best, Sir Ralph. Of course, I don't want to say anything unofficial, but there's a chance. You see, there was provocation—great provocation; and although certainly an innocent man was allowed to swing for it, yet it's a very genteel case, and juries often stretch a point when an old gentleman is brought before them, especially with white hair. I have known white hair do a deal more for a man than innocence, so you mustn't be too down about it, Sir."

With many a consolatory speech of this description, Barman whiled away the time. The boat soon reached the shore and they disembarked.

"I shan't take you to the station, Sir Ralph, as we should meet a number of unpleasant people there,—drunkards and such like cases. No, Sir, you shall come off direct to my lodgings, and I'll soon make you as comfortable as can be."

With this, they reached a small house in one of the back streets. The detective produced a latch-key, opened the door, and with his prisoner made good an entrance.

*   *   *   *   *   *

After Leopold had bidden Sir Ralph farewell, he returned to London, and took up his abode once again at Royal Chambers.

" Thank God !" he murmured, as he threw himself into an arm-chair, "my father's saved—saved, and by me! What a fearful crime have I escaped. Parricide—great Heavens, parricide !"

And he sat looking into the fire, with his thoughts far away.

" And Florence, poor child !"

Was there any hope in the thought ? Florence was a widow now, and— He scarcely dared pursue the theme. Mind,

he had been twice deceived, and yet here he
was (fool, poor fool!) building up a gorgeous,
magnificent castle—in the air!

London in October is painfully dull. If
any one is anybody he finds it particularly
slow. No balls, no operas, "no nothing!"
The club is as deserted as the park, and,
with the exception of a couple of million or
so, there remains not a soul in town. Royal
Chambers was of course deserted; in fact,
had fallen into the hands of the whitewashers.
Marlborough House, with its solitary sentinel
(telling of the absence of the Prince and
Princess), scarcely boasted a visitor, and as
for St. James's Street, it looked like a tho-
roughfare in the City of the Dead!

Leopold dressed and walked into the club.

The hall-porter regarded him with surprise—with disgust, as if he had been a
plebeian ghost. What right had he to be in
town in October?—that was the point.

" Any letters for me?"

" No, Sir, none."

" Anybody in the club ?"

" Only one gentleman, Sir—a new member—Mr. Marcus Perks, Sir. Barrister, I believe, Sir."

Leopold walked on, passed the swing doors of the hall, passed the swing doors of the morning-room, and found himself in the apartment devoted to light literature and journalism. Reading the 'Pall Mall Gazette' in solitary grandeur was Mr. Marcus Perks. Leopold addressed him.

" I think we've met before ?"

Perks stared at him for a moment through an eye-glass, and said,

" I know your face perfectly well—perfectly well. Stay, didn't I once defend you in a case of malicious libel, or was it a divorce affair ?"

" No," replied Leopold with a smile. " I have never had the honour of being your client. My name is Lawson—Leopold Lawson."

"Oh, to be sure!" cried Perks, shaking hands warmly. "Are you a member here?"

"Yes."

"I rather like the place. Very chatty and sociable, and the best situation in London. Are you feeding here?"

"I think so."

"Shall we feed together?"

"By all means."

And the two young men proceeded to the dining-room to order their dinner. In due course the soup appeared, and the two friends were called to the banquet.

"Singular case to-day," said Marcus, when they were seated. "I had to prosecute a Government official,—no less a man than the Controller-in-Chief of the Paupers' Property Office!"

"What, Mr. Cumberland Kenny?"

"That's the fellow's name. He's been committing forgery to an alarming extent. Forged the name of half his clerks to a number of bills. The bills were renewed from time to time by a bill-discounter, Mr. Moses Melchisideck, until Kenny could pay no longer, and then Moses (who's a Christian by the way) came down upon him. Do you know anything of Kenny ?"

"Not much; but I will tell you who does,—the man you recommended to me years ago, John Barman, the detective."

"John Barman—ah, yes. I heard from him the other day. He wrote to me to say that he was about your affair. You have been successful ?"

"Yes—very—successful !"

"Well, I suppose I ought to congratulate you; but I can't. I don't believe somehow in amateur justice. It's all very well for novels, but in real life, why, the thing becomes a bore."

And then they began to talk about other things.

After dinner they went into the smoking-room for cigars and coffee.

"By Jove," said Marcus, reading from the last edition of the 'Globe,' "there was a fearful storm at the mouth of the Mersey last night. A lot of ships had to put back to Liverpool. The 'Columbia' lost her foremast, and had to be towed back in an awfully disabled state. Hallo, what's the matter? You look as pale as a ghost."

Leopold was fearfully agitated, but he speedily regained his composure.

"Nothing," he answered; "nothing. I only feel a little faint, that's all. I think I shall go home."

And with this, he shook hands with Perks, and left the club.

"'The Columbia' returned to Liverpool, and Barman there! Great Heavens, my father,—my father!"

As for Perks, he rang the bell, and ordered the waiter to bring the 'Tomahawk.'

"I always read it when I'm in a bad temper," he said. "It helps me to swear!"

* * * * * *

A room with bars to the windows. A room with plain furniture. A room more like a prison than a palace.

Two men occupied this room, Sir Ralph and John Barman. The old man sat in an easy-chair apparently unconscious of the presence of the detective. He had not said a word for hours,—his gaze was fixed upon the wall with a meaningless stare.

"You are nice company, Sir Ralph, I must say," said Barman, in high displeasure. "There was a lot of good in my cautioning you not to commit yourself,—wasn't there? Yah, I've no patience with you! You're not half a man!"

The baronet seemed not to have heard this *very* respectful address; at least, he made no reply to it.

"Well," continued Barman, "I shall leave you to yourself. I don't think you can do yourself much harm, as I searched you before you came in. Better not leave you the poker, perhaps. Good night."

And the detective took up the fire-irons, went out, and locked the door after him.

Sir Ralph did not notice for some time his absence. At last, however, he gradually became conscious of the fact, and then his head fell upon his breast, and his nature thawed into a flood of tears. It was pitiable to watch this old man in his agony.

"What shall I do?" he cried in a frenzy of despair; "what shall I do? They will hang me—they will kill me! and I can't save myself—I can't save myself!"

And then despair gave place to fury, and he tried to kill himself. He looked about him for the means of self-destruction, but (thanks to the precautions of the detective) could find nothing. Soon the fit left him, and then he was once more reduced to an utterly hopeless and utterly strengthless despair.

And from this state he gradually dropped into a broken slumber, and he dreamed a dream.

He dreamed that he was carried, screaming and protesting, into a court of justice.

It seemed to him to be like the court in which Lawson had been tried. He was placed at the dock, and then found that he could not move, could not utter a word. Round about him was a sea of faces—faces of the friends he had known during all his life. And as he looked at the faces they frowned upon him, and he trembled before their glances. But among those faces, there was one who returned his gaze with tearful eyes,—a face that was full of sorrow—it was the face of his mother! And as he stood trembling in the dock, he felt the presence of some unearthly visitant near him. He turned his head round, and there, close beside him, stood Lady Ruthven,—his dead wife, risen from the ocean, with the sea-

weed fantastically grouped about her shroud.
And as he looked at her pale lifeless face,
she took his hand within her own, and a
cold shiver shook his feeble frame from head
to foot.

And then he dreamed that the trial began
—the trial of the living and the dead. He
heard the words of the witnesses as they
proved fact after fact. He listened to the
tick of the clock that stood over the jury
box, and it ticked out, "He is the murderer, he is the murderer!" He looked at
the graining of the panels, and there again
he made out the words, "He is the murderer. He is the murderer!" In the cracks
on the ceiling he could trace some writing,
and the same sentence once more appeared.
And the trial went on, and he knew that
every one in that court knew him to be
guilty.

And now the judge summed up, and he
heard the death words of the jury, and there

was a mighty shout, and the court rang with, "He is the murderer, he is the murderer!"

Still he could not say a word. And his dead wife left him now, floating away in the evening dusk, left him to his fate—left him to die!

And then he heard the judge speaking, and asking him why he should not be hanged by the neck until he was dead, and then his voice returned to him, and he began to reply.

To his horror he found that he was condemning himself—that his words were those of self-accusation. And when he had done speaking, another shout of "He is the murderer, he is the murderer!" rent the air. And then he knew that the judge was passing upon him sentence of death.

It was all over now, and he was in a dungeon all alone. The morning was breaking, and he knew that it was the day on which he had to die. And he tried to pray, and mocking sounds filled his ears; it seemed as if the cell were tenanted with devils. And he heard the clock strike six, and he had but two hours to live!

And now he saw his past life, as it were, like a picture unfurled before him. Sin upon sin, wrong upon wrong, rose up in evidence against him. And he tried to pray, and his prayers once more were drowned in mocking laughter. And he nearly died of sorrow and despair, and then the clock struck seven, and he had but one hour to live!

And now he seemed to act once more in the scene of Raymond's murder. The discovery and the death followed close upon one another. And then he heard the mocking voices telling him that John Lawson had been accused, and that he, Ralph Ruthven, had committed a double murder by allowing an innocent man to be hanged. And then he saw Leopold stretching out his hand and pointing to a rope. And the clock struck eight, and he knew his hour had come !

At last he was in the hands of the hangman. He was conducted through the prison, and now the moment had arrived when he must meet the yelling crowd. He walked up to the scaffold, and then fell on his knees and implored forgiveness and deliverance. Those who listened to him turned away, and the hangman touched him and whispered to him that his conduct was unworthy of him, that he should act like a man.

And then he tried to scream, but his voice had gone and he could not utter a word. And then he felt that he was being carried on to the scaffold, and that in a few moments he would be dead !

And now he stood looking at a sea of upturned faces, who jeered at him and challenged him to "die game," and laughed horrid laughter, and yelled at him, and among those faces he saw a vision of hell !

R 2

And he tried once more to pray with all his might—with all his soul. But the sounds of the hideous laughter and devilish songs flooded his ears, and he had thought—mind —for nothing else. And he shrieked again in his mortal agony!

And now he was in darkness, and he felt the fatal rope about his neck.

Wild with horror, he made one supreme effort to escape, there was a strange agony, he tried to breathe, and he shrieked!

*　　*　　*　　*　　*　　*

There was some confusion in John Barman's lodgings. He had been called up early by the sound of a piercing scream, and he had had to send out for a doctor. He was talking to this doctor now.

" Oh, yes, natural causes no doubt,—a fit at his time of life would of course be serious."

" Well, doctor, I thank you very much. Will you just step into the parlour to drink a glass of wine and sign the necessary certificate."

The doctor complied, and the two worthies walked into the state apartment. As they combined a little business with some mild carousal, a cab drew up to the door, and a young man jumped out and rang the bell.

"This is Mr. Barman's house," said he, hurriedly, when the servant appeared.

"Yes, Sir," answered the maid, and the matter was taken out of her hands by the appearance of the detective himself. Barman looked very pale and grave.

"My father!" was all the young man cried.

Barman led the way to the baronet's room, and allowed the son to enter. Leopold started, turned deadly pale, and then flung himself beside the bed and covered Sir Ralph's hand with kisses.

"Don't distress yourself, my dear young gentleman," said the doctor, who had fol-

lowed Barman into the chamber of death
"It may be a comfort for you to learn tha
your relative or friend died of apoplexy, an
without any pain.   He must have passe
away as calmly as a summer's evening!"

CHAPTER XI.

ON THE SHORE OF THE GREAT HEREAFTER.

A COLD, a pitiable cold night in the London streets. Mid-winter—"jolly Christmas," with bills, and writs, and starvation. Theatrically beautiful, a very mine of wealth for the well-fed, well-paid novelist, practically a sure but lingering death to the poor forlorn houseless beggar. The publishers' shops teemed with jovial "annuals," covered with wonderful pictures of holly and mistletoe and all sorts of good cheer; the workhouse door was besieged by numbers of miserable wretches, seeking shelter from the sleet and

snow,— a miserable night—a very miserable
night.

It was six o'clock, and little crowds were
gathering round the pit and gallery entrances
of the theatres,—roast-chestnut men, with
glowing cans of coke and noses tinted by
gin, were driving a roaring trade, while
oranges and sweetstuffs were certainly at a
discount. In one of the houses in the Waterloo Road a group was collected in the parlour, consisting of two ugly children and a
delicate-looking woman of about four-and-
twenty. The children (two girls) were
gathering up their books, and the woman
was putting on her bonnet and shawl.

" Miss Wood," said the elder of the girls,
" Mar wants to see you partickler before
you go—very partickler—you are to go in
to her."

" Yes, Miss Wood," cried the other child.
" You're in a nice row, I can tell you ? You
won't be turned away ! Oh, dear no !"

"Don't you be vulgar, Miss," exclaimed the other child. "You know Mar said we weren't to say anything about it."

"I ain't vulgar."

"Yes, you are—isn't she, Miss Wood?"

The poor pale-faced woman had listened to this little conversation with resignation and sorrow. Now that she was ready to go, she kissed her two pupils and said,

"Good bye, my dears. I hope I am not bidding you good bye for the last time. God bless you."

And she went downstairs to their mother's room, which was under the level of the pavement.

"Julia, ain't you glad she's going? Nasty, tiresome, weak thing, wasn't she?"

"Yes, Madge. We shan't have no work until Mar finds another."

"Say, shall have no work,—shan't have no work is vulgar."

"Shan't!"

"Very well, Miss. Then I shall tell Mar of your stealing the jam."

"Will you, Miss? Then take that."

Combat of two.

In the meanwhile the poor woman had descended to the private apartments of the "Mar" in question, and stood in her august presence.

"Miss Wood," began the matron,—she was fat, wheezy, and of the cheesemonger persuasion, "you and I can't get on, so you must go. You know I ain't a lady of many words, and that's the plain English of it."

"In what have I failed to give you satisfaction?" asked Miss Wood in a weak voice.

"Well, you ain't strong enough for the place. Them girls of mine require a deal of looking after, and you can't do it,—at least to my liking. Why only the other day you let 'em break a milk jug."

"I have done my best, and—"

"Your best ain't good enough for me," interrupted the matron snappishly. "There, let's have no more words about it. Here, take your last week's money and go."

She threw a few shillings on the table and bounced out of the room.

The poor girl (she looked no more than a girl) took up the paltry sum, drew her shawl more closely round her, sighed, and left the house.

"Heaven help me," she cried. "What shall I do! Oh, what shall I do!"

She walked on desperately to the bridge and murmured,

"I cannot live. Driven from door to door, homeless, friendless, would it not be better to die at once?"

And she walked on with a quicker step towards the river. City men on their way to the Waterloo Station stared at her as she passed them by. One, indeed, spoke to a policeman, and pointed her out to him.

" I'd advise you to keep your eye upon that woman—she looks desperate," he said.

" She's gone out of my beat already," said A. S. 174, looking after her.

" And I have to catch the 6.10 train."

So she was permitted to continue her journey without interruption.

She walked on hurriedly to the bridge, and after paying the toll, stood beside the parapet looking down into the river. The lights were reflected in the dark, black water, the lights of the great city, so bright on the shore, so faint and vague in the flowing river. And as she looked into the murky stream beneath the bridge she thought,

" Is it not better that it should end now? How can I hope to live with starvation gnawing at my poor despairing heart? And even if I do linger on, what do I live for? Hopeless, friendless, futureless! It is only one jump, one minute of agony, and then a long hereafter of rest, perfect rest; surely God would not punish me, knowing all."

And she stood looking into the river, and seeking comfort in its cold, repellent bosom.

As she stood thus, a man walked on to the bridge. He moved moodily along, his head bowed down upon his chest, his right hand pressed to his heart. He was dressed in deep mourning. He came up to her, and watched her as he saw her leaning over the parapet so sadly. As he watched, she seemed to have made up her mind, and to have determined upon suicide.

It was only then that he touched her. He laid his hand gently upon her arm, and said, "What are you going to do?"

When she heard his voice she started and trembled. She hid her poor pale face in her threadbare shawl, and tried to avoid recognition, and then she stood quite still— motionless as a statue.

"What would you do?" he repeated in

a dull, desperate voice. "Give up the fight with fate! Murder the soul that God has given you!"

She thrilled at his voice, she thrilled at his touch.

"Come, poor woman, the world has used you badly, and you are mad and weary of life? Well, the world has used me badly, and I look upon death as a longed-for deliverance. Come, sister, let us argue it out —life or death,—and then let us seek the great Hereafter together. See, we stand upon the edge of Hell,—shall we take the plunge?"

And he pointed to the river, as it flowed coldly, silently, darkly beneath them.

She shuddered at his words, but was silent.

"Tell me, have you staked your all upon love and lost? Have you been deceived, and has the deception driven you mad?"

She was silent, but the tears were flowing fast.

"Tell me, sister, has your one hope died out? Has your only chance of happiness been lost for ever and ever?"

She was wringing her hands now, but her face was hidden from him.

"All this has happened to me, sister! And *there* is deliverance—there is rest until the day of judgment!"

And again he pointed to the river.

"Come, tell me your story—tell me if you've been happier than I?"

"Oh, no! no!" she sobbed out.

"Tell me, has your past been so bitter, so very bitter, that your future can be, *must* be misery? Yes, it is so! One more question —have you anything to live for?"

"Nothing!"

"Nor I, sister, nor I!" cried the man with a wild laugh. "Then why should we live—you and I? Surely it would be better for both of us to die!"

And he took her cold, unresisting hand

within his own.   She turned round, and for
the first time showed her face, then she
cried in piteous accents,

"Oh, Leopold, Leopold, have we come to
this?"

"Florence!   Great Heaven—Florence!"

Thus they met once more—met beside the
dreadful river—that river that flows on—on
even unto Death!

CHAPTER XII.

DEATH AND CUPID!

A DARKENED room. A nurse sat by the side of the bed. Every now and then she rose from her chair, and looked at the pale face of the poor girl over whom she watched.

"Not much life in her, poor thing," she murmured. "I know the face too well; it's all over with her."

And then there was a gentle knock at the door, and a staid old gentleman walked into the room. It was the doctor. He asked a few questions of the woman in attendance, and looked at the patient. Then he shook his head and whispered,

"I fear there's a change for the worse, poor thing."

And after a few directions he left the room as he had entered it, silently and sorrowfully. When he had descended the stairs, he was accosted by Leopold Lawson, who waited impatiently for his verdict.

"Well?"

"No hope, I fear," said the doctor. "She is gradually sinking; if she has any friends, you had better communicate with them."

"Is there no hope?"

"I am afraid none. She may linger on for a few days. She may die to-night; but unless a miracle be worked she cannot recover."

Leopold sighed heavily, shook hands with the good physician, and turned his head away to avoid showing his tears.

"There is always *some* hope in every case," continued the doctor in a comforting tone. "Still I should not be doing my duty if I did not reveal to you my forebodings."

And thus they parted.

Leopold entered the parlour, and throwing himself into an arm-chair, buried his face in his hands, and wept aloud. He had recovered his lost love, only to see her die !—die, and he unable to save her ! He was unconscious of everything save his great grief.

By-and-by there was a knock at the door, and the nurse entered.

" She is awake, Sir," she said, " and is crying for you. Poor dear young lady ! I am afraid it will soon be over."

Leopold made a supreme effort to regain his composure. He asked,

" Does she know where she is ?"

" Yes, Sir. I told her how you brought her here, and how sorry we all were to see her so ill, and she called out that she must see you at once before she died."

Leopold rose from his chair, and silently left the room. He ascended the stairs ; he stopped for a moment at the door of the chamber of death, and prayed to his God to give him strength to preserve his composure. Then he gently opened the door and went in.

" Florence !"

" Oh, Leopold, Leopold!" cried the dying girl in a faint voice, " you have come to me at last—you have forgiven me ?"

" Forgiven you, my darling—my own, dear love ! What have I to forgive you ? Oh, Florence, my poor love ! It is I who must ask forgiveness ! It is I who must implore your pardon. What right had I to cross your path ? What right had I to have caused you a moment's pain ?"

And he knelt down beside the bed, and his tear-stained face bent over the poor thin hand stretched out to him.

" Oh, Leopold, I've been mad, been wicked ! But God has blessed me in once more letting me see you—oh, darling, oh, my love!" And she passed her hand through his hair caressingly.

Leopold answered her words with his sobs.

"You can forgive me, darling? You can really forgive me now that I am dying? You are not angry with me now?"

"Angry, Florence! Oh, my love, how could I be angry with you? I never have had one thought of aught else than love, darling, in my heart! Angry! Had you killed me, darling, I would have blessed you with my last breath!"

"And I have killed you, my darling. I have killed you, your happiness, your hope. Killed you, oh, my darling—my dear, dear love!"

She drew away her hands and raised them to her eyes, and her tears fell fast through the poor thin fingers.

Leopold, by an almost superhuman effort of will, stopped weeping, and said in a broken voice,

"My dear child, you must not distress yourself. To know that you were happy gave me great comfort. I lived only for you. Your happiness was my first wish, my only care. As for me, I have lived very happily. I have not felt the wound so— so—"

And here his lips trembled, and he broke down.

She took his hand once more, and now *she* was calm, and it was he who had lost self-command.

"Dear Leopold, I want to tell you something. It has been on my mind to tell you over and over again. But I loved you, darling, and I was alive then,—now I am sinking into the grave, and must soon die. Don't cry, dear, it is better for all of us that it should be so. Better, much better."

And she patted his head with her hand, as a mother would have comforted a suffering child.

"I want you, darling, when I am dead, to marry one who has loved you for years. She has been so true to you, dear—always your friend. She it was who, in spite of the great love she bore you, tried, oh, so hard, to turn my wicked, frivolous heart towards you. She it was who fought your battles and defended you from all the attacks of your enemies. She who has sacrificed her own happiness for mine. Dear Edith, my own darling sister !"

" Edith !"

" Yes, Edith. You must marry her; you will soon learn to love her, everybody loves her, and you will be happy. Oh, I shall die so calmly if I can only believe that I leave behind me a legacy of love. You will try to like her ; will you not, Leopold ?"

The young man bowed his head and then she continued,

" And now, Leopold, before I die let me tell you why we never married."

"No, Florence darling. Let us forget the past."

"He forced me; he threatened me with my family's disgrace; my adopted father's death. And I was weak and cruel and wrong, and I accepted him, but I never ceased from loving you. And oh, Leopold, I have been so punished — so cruelly punished!"

"I know, dear, I know all now. He is dead, let us say no more about him."

And then they spoke in whispers—it seemed to be that the past of broken faith had gone, and that they had returned to the time when they were first engaged. Leopold knelt by the bed with her hand in his, his eye fixed on hers. They talked as unreservedly as they were wont to talk of old; both were happy, contented, at rest.

Thus the hours passed. Florence growing weaker and weaker. Leopold at last noticed the growing change; as he gazed upon her face he saw death—cold, horrible death!

She saw the horror in his eyes and quickly read his meaning.

"Oh, Leopold, I am dying! Don't let me die, darling! I want to live for you!"

He drew his face to hers, and kissed her poor thin lips.

"Save me, Leopold, save me! I must not die—I cannot die! I have found you now, Leopold, I want to live!"

He soothed her, although his tears flowed quickly; he soothed her with a trembling hand and broken voice.

"You have forgiven me, darling?"

He pressed her hand.

"You love me, darling?"

He kissed her lips. She threw her arms round his neck.

And thus lip to lip, with perfect love for one another in their hearts, they parted. He to dwell in the world and bear his sorrow for evermore—to live among men, and yet to share few of their pleasures—to know none of their joys. And she—ah, her poor erring spirit had winged its flight to a more merciful world than this—a more beautiful world than this—to a world where laws are love and tears are never known.

Lip to lip, so they parted. Parted, yes for ever—for ever until the great hereafter.

The morning broke, and yet he knelt beside the bed with her cold dead hand clasped within his own !

End of Book IV.

The Epilogue.

A LEGACY OF LOVE!

CHAPTER I.

HOME.

THE spring has come. Stelstead is glorious with bright green leaves—the birds sing—the sun shines—nature rejoices in her new lease of life. Our little village is very much changed. The Grammar School has new buildings—masters' houses of red brick and white stone, a chapel, and, wonder of wonders, a gymnasium! Then a little railway (a lawyers' railway it may be called, as it has been the cause of a hundred squabbles) is here running off towards Dunmow and other large towns. Then there are some

modern villas built with a view to accommo-
dating rich city men with country tastes, and
actually a new church. The only thing
that seems to be unchanged (for even the
shops have new fronts, gorgeous with plate
glass and burnished brass) is Jas Samson's
little shop. The old cobbler, although an
advanced Liberal in theory, is in practice a
confirmed Conservative.

As we look at him for the last time, he is
sitting in his work-room, cheery and bright-
hearted, mending his boots and shoes. He
has a visitor. Father Dutton stands at the
door, talking to him.

"To-day, Sir; you say to-day!" exclaims
Jas, for the third time with a bright smile.

"Yes, Mr. Samson, he comes back to-day.
He has tired of travelling, and returns to
the home of his ancestors."

"Not much difficulty about proving his
right to the title, I suppose, Sir?"

"No, Mr. Samson, not much. You see,

Sir Ralph had left it cut-and-dried in his will. His return will be a good thing for the county."

"And what will become of Miss Edith now, Sir? You know she can't keep looking after the house now that he's come back."

The priest smiled.

"There may be a pleasant future for her,' —who knows? At present, however, I believe she intends returning to her mother's family."

"She's a good woman, bless her, Sir. The poor will miss her when she's gone."

"Let's hope, then, she won't go."

It was now the cobbler's turn to smile.

"Ah, Sir, I see what you mean. Well, I hope it may be so. Shall we take a walk round the garden, Sir? I've got some new shrubs that I think are beauties, Sir. Will you make me proud enough to have a look at them, Sir?"

"Well, Mr. Samson, I have a spare quarter of an hour. Lead on."

And they go in together. Two good men. Good, because they live plain, spotless lives. *Sans peur et sans reproche.* Of different creeds, and yet both (let us trust) equally blest. I have sketched them with faulty pencil, I know. Thank Heaven they are alive at this moment, and do not require my pen to testify to their merits. Bid them adieu, my reader, for we see them in these pages for the last time.

Farewell, priest and cobbler. Priest, pure and simple; cobbler, simple and pure. Unlike, and yet like. They have one thing in common; the nobility of nature that marks the Christian gentleman.

*   *   *   *   *   *

All is preparation in Stelstead Hall. The new baronet is expected every minute. The servants are gorgeous in new liveries, the maids spruce in splendid caps and natty aprons. Every one is greatly excited; for is it not the day of Sir Leopold Ruthven's (7th baronet) return to his native place? Is it not a time for feasting and merry-making?

And yet there is one sad face—the face of a very beautiful woman—the face of Edith Ruthven, who waits in the library the return of her cousin to his new home.

"Here is his last letter," she says, "let me read it again. '*I have decided upon coming back at once, dear cousin. I shall probably be at Stelstead by the 16th. I can't tell you how grateful I am for your kind consent to my request. I am so glad that you made up your mind to stay at Stelstead. I look forward to seeing you with much pleasure.*' Look forward to seeing me! Look forward to seeing me!"

And she sighs, and her thoughts are far away from Stelstead,—far away back into the past.

And now there is the noise of wheels, and the trampling of horses is heard on the gravel walk. Then the noise ceases, and there is a silence.

A silence followed by a mighty shout—a shout from the throats of scores of labourers and ploughboys, and women and children, a shout loud and long, as an English shout should be.

The shout comes from the Ruthven tenants, welcoming the new baronet to his own.

Leopold descends from his carriage. He is now a grave man, but still there is rest in his eye, a smile upon his calm lips. He has been wounded sadly, but the wounds have healed, and though the scars are still seen, he no longer feels their once cruel smart. Time has taken compassion upon him, and while making him older, has carried away sorrow and care.

Leopold lifts his hat in acknowledgment to the cheer of his tenantry, and then turning to a bowing, cringing servant, asks,

"Is Miss Ruthven within?"

"She is in the library, Sir Leopold."

And the wanderer returns home.

CHAPTER II.

THE GOOD SAMARITAN.

EDITH sits in the library looking out of the window upon the park before her. Her cheek rests upon her hand, her arm upon the window-sill.

The door is opened softly and a man enters the room. He approaches her.

"Edith!"

She turns quickly round, and her hand is clasped within his own. A thrill of pleasure makes her tremble.

"Edith," he continues. "I want to ask you a question."

She looks down and waits to hear his voice once more.

"I have lost my youth, Edith. I am a grave lonely man. I have travelled and have at last found peace in forgetfulness. I am very lonely, Edith; I have no kith or kin, not a friend in the world! I have loved you as a sister, as a dear, dear sister."

She is silent, but her bosom heaves with emotion.

"While I have been away," he continues, "I have grown a cold, grave man. I have thought and thought, and my whole nature is changed. I have learned to appreciate you at your just value,—I have learned to love as you should be loved."

He pauses for a moment and then continues. "I ask you Edith—dear Edith, can you love me? Can you help me to forget the past? Can you share my fate? Will you be my wife?"

She whispers an answer, and is clasped in

his arms. A smile of supreme rest and thankfulness illumines her face.

"My dear, dear love," she murmurs, "I have loved you from the first."

He kisses her forehead, and they stand at the open window looking out upon the bright landscape before them. The sun sinks, and still their whispered words continue. The stars begin to twinkle in the clear cloudless sky.

At last Edith murmurs "Florence," and her eyes are fixed upon his.

"It was her wish, darling," he replies; and he sighs, "Poor Florence."

Tears gather in her eyes, and she repeats after him,

"Poor Florence!"

And they stand bathed in the moonlight, and in their hearts are enshrined two sweet words—words full of good omens for the future—"Love" and "Hope."

———

My tale is over.

Before bidding my readers farewell, however, it is only courteous that I should sketch, for his or her benefit, the story of those characters who have filled a minor place on the broad canvas of my wild design. Those who wish to learn the fate of John Barman and the rest may read my last words; those who do not, can close the book at once. The details are perhaps not very interesting.

First then, John Barman. He is still alive, I believe. If you have, fair reader, behaved badly, or, stern reader, are of a jealous temperament, our friend the detective is the very man for you. He will help you out of trouble or into trouble, as you please. Of late he has been in great spirits. He declares that things are looking up splendidly—that crime is really on the increase. And as for the Divorce Court, that it is the wonder and pride of the nineteenth century!

Mr. Cumberland Kenny was sent a couple of years ago to Portland for a little matter of forging a gentleman's signature. I don't know if he is there *now*, but his place knows him not at the Paupers' Property Office.

It is whispered in official circles that there are many clerks in the " P. P. O." who would gladly change places with their quondam chief!

Mr. Marcus Perks is even now a Q.C.— some day he will be a judge.

Mr. Moses Melchisideck still grows rich, but he is quite a changed man. He has turned " serious ;" has recognized the errors of his ways, and never lends money now— under sixty-five per cent. !

The proprietor of the Ruthven Arms is still a widower. He preferred a quiet gentlemanly strait-waistcoat to the bonds of wedlock! He is living now somewhere in the neighbourhood of Hanwell!

As for Leopold, we leave him happy.

Poor fellow, we have seen him in the hands of the "thieves"—is it not gratifying to notice that he has at last found a "good Samaritan"—a pretty one too—to comfort and to succour him?

And now, reader, I lay down my pen. The performance is over—the puppets are in my hands for the last time—I let go of their strings and see—they fall to the ground.

Pull down the curtain, turn out the lamps, —my little play is done.

THE END.